THE OSCAR SPEECH

THE OSCAR SPEECH

A Two-Timing, Double-Dealing,
Poetically-Profane, but Infinitely Charming
Oscar Nominee Will Do Anything to Win!

DAVID CREPS

The Oscar Speech
A Two-Timing, Double-Dealing, Poetically-Profane, but Infinitely Charming Oscar Nominee Will Do Anything to Win!

David Creps

Published by Boogie Woogie Books and David Creps
ISBN: 978-1-7354725-8-4

FREE BONUS BOOK!

Get a **FREE** copy of David Creps' hilarious television pilot:

ONE MORE FOR THE ROAD

This is the story of the Cranberrys–a small group of eccentric individuals living on a breathtakingly beautiful mountainside near Lake Tahoe.

The center of activity is Randy Cranberry. Relentlessly optimistic, he truly believes that he has written a movie script that holds the solution for "preventing the human species from continuing down its current, rapid, and obvious path to total and everlasting destruction." He spends a part of every day strategizing on how to get this script into Steven Spielberg's hands.

Libby Cranberry is Randy's wife, a sixty-five-year-old Chinese woman who claims she is less than sixty-two-and-a-half years of age. She is also notably superstitious and–to her husband's constant dismay–is more than willing to give him a plentiful amount of unsolicited advice, at any hour, day or night.

And then there is Penrod Cranberry, who is three years younger than his brother Randy. One might describe him as a dapper old hippie who lives alone in a two-story, aspen-tree cabin, constructed on the large flatbed of a 1946 Dodge truck straddling a beautiful mountain stream.

Penrod's primary interest in life is the same as Randy's: to make the most insulting remark possible . . . as often as possible . . . to each other.

Get your FREE copy of *One More for the Road* here:

www.BoogieWoogieBooks.com/bonus

This book is dedicated to the first person who reads it and says, "I read it, I love it! The two principal characters would be perfect roles for Meryl Streep and Frances McDormand, who are both friends of mine, and I would be honored to deliver your book into their hands!!!"

CHAPTER ONE

Several years after the pandemic, three dealers, Johnny, Monty, and Bob, all between thirty and forty years of age, stand at a 'dead' craps table, bullshitting.

Johnny inquires, "Everybody going to Myrna's Oscar party?"

Monty, the stickman, answers without diverting his attention from a cocktail waitress as she crosses the casino floor to deliver drinks to a group of blackjack players at the far end of the pit. "Not me."

Johnny asks, "Where you gonna be?"

Monty turns back to the dice game. "Home. My wife's entire family is coming over to watch it at our house. And I gotta feed the fuckers."

Bob enters the conversation. "I'm going over to Rob's. You guys ever see his TV? It's about eight feet across. Glare resistant. High definition. Ten billion pixels. All that shit. It's great. If a star's got a pimple, you'll be able to see it." He then directs himself specifically to Johnny, "You wanna go over to Rob's with me?"

Johnny, who appears a little less well-kempt than the other dealers, answers, "Actually, I'm probably not even gonna watch it. I'm off that Monday and Tuesday, and I was thinking maybe I'll go camping up at Tahoe for a couple days."

Bob scoffs, "Oh bullshit. You'll be sitting right there in front of the TV, just like the rest of us, waiting for some millionaire movie star to screw up in front of twenty billion people."

CHAPTER TWO

Five hundred miles away, the evening vibe is settling on Malibu as the surf pounds the shore below the array of heavy beams and soft cushions of the Swanky Shampane residence.

A quivering dance of flames throws out is warmth from a massive rock fireplace. Through a panorama of huge windows, the sun slides slowly into the Pacific Ocean.

There is only one decorative item on any of the polished mahogany walls inside this home: an expensively framed sign, hand-written in red crayon, is featured above the liquor shelf behind the bar: "When all that life seems to be offering you is one big lemon, grab the sonofabitch and make yourself some fuckin' lemonade."

Swanky, a very attractive woman somewhere between fifty and seventy, walks into the room and sits on a heavily padded bar stool. She pours herself a drink, then makes a call on the speakerphone.

A man answers, "Hello."

Swanky takes a sip of her drink before speaking, "Hello, Stanley."

There is a brief pause before the conversation continues.

"Hello, Swanky. Nice to hear your voice."

Swanky smiles. "You're a lying sack of shit, Stan. It's not at all nice for you to hear my voice. The last time you heard my voice it cost you approximately two million dollars . . . per year."

Stanley's voice loses its charm, "Whaddaya want, Swanky?"

Swanky sips again. "Purely business, Stanley. Nothing's changed. I still hate your guts. But, I will do business with you."

"All right. And I'm perfectly willing to do business with you, as long as you understand that I will always consider you to be the lousiest bitch on the planet."

Swanky smiles, "No problem."

"What's the business?"

"I want Victoria Blaine to mention my name in her Oscar speech."

Stanley bursts a laugh. "Are you outta your mind? Why would Victoria Blaine mention you in her Oscar speech?"

"A trade-off. If she wins, she mentions me, if I win, I mention her."

Stanley delights in having Swanky in a position where he

can insult her with sincerity, "Sounds like Victoria would be getting the short end of that deal."

"Fuck you, Stanley."

Stanley ignores her crassness. "And what if neither one of you win?"

"I also want you to make that same arrangement for me with the other three nominees."

Stanley dismisses this ridiculous antic, "In the first place, Swanky, I couldn't possibly arrange something like that. And in the second place, even if I could, I wouldn't."

"Stanley, even though I made you look like a second-rate player when I left you and went with Idors . . . I am now thinking of leaving Idors and returning to you."

Swanky stirs her drink to give Stanley time to consider the ramifications of her remark. She then continues, "How do you suppose that would be perceived? Like Idors couldn't get the job done, so I returned to CCA?

"That would kind of push your reputation back up to where it used to be, wouldn't it? Not to mention the two million bucks a year you'd once again be making off me." Swanky gives Stanley a moment before continuing, "Think it over, Stanley, and call me back."

Swanky presses the speakerphone off, walks over and sits on the couch in front of the fireplace, takes a sip of her drink, picks a copy of *Architectural Digest* off the coffee table, and proceeds to thumb through it.

CHAPTER THREE

Back at the casino, the same three dealers stand at the same dead craps table.

A fourth dealer, Fred, walks up to the table and runs his finger several inches down the stickman's back: proper procedure for dice dealers returning from their break.

Monty hands him the 'stick,' moves around the table, and steps into Johnny's spot. Johnny moves over a few steps into Bob's spot, and Bob goes on break.

Fred speaks to Johnny during this rotation, "Hey, I was just talking to Jerry, and he said he got your 'Wednesday-Thursday.'"

Johnny nods. "Yep."

Fred seems surprised to have this news confirmed. "Why in the hell would you give up a 'Wednesday-Thursday' to get a 'Monday-Tuesday?'"

Monty interjects, "He had his days changed because he didn't want to have the same days off as Rita, because then he might see her someplace with her new boyfriend . . . and that would make him sad."

Fred looks over to Johnny to confirm or deny. "You broke up with Rita?"

Johnny shrugs. "She broke up with me."

Fred probes for details. "No shit. How come?"

Monty interjects again, "She said he was an idiot, and she was tired of being an idiot's girlfriend."

Fred looks at Johnny. "No shit?"

Johnny reluctantly confirms it. "Yeah, I guess that was sorta the gist of it."

Monty fills in a slight gap, "And also there was that part about Stewart, her aerobics instructor."

Fred hesitates. "That moron with the tattoo across his back . . . of a rat taking a crap?"

Monty confirms the worst. "Yep, that's her new guy. And that's why Johnny got his days off changed. And that's why he's thinking that he might not go to Myrna's Oscar party. Because, maybe Rita and her new guy might show up. Right, Johnny?"

Johnny pushes back, "Wrong again Monty, as usual."

Monty doesn't want to beat this dead horse, but he is actually curious, "Then why wouldn't you go? You've been going to her Oscar party ever since she started having them. Why wouldn't you go this year?"

Johnny is ready to drop the subject. "No reason. Just don't feel like it."

Monty needs just a little more. "Right. You don't feel like it. Instead, you feel like snow-shoeing into the mountains around Tahoe and camping out for two sub-zero nights, during avalanche season."

Fred is struck with a thought: "Hey Johnny, you know what you should do. You should talk to my cousin Ralph. He's got a limousine, and he rents it for twenty-five hundred dollars to take people to the Academy Awards.

"I'm not shittin' ya. Twenty-five hundred bucks for one night. He does it every year. They don't have enough limos in L.A. for all the people that want to take limos that night.

"However, at the moment, my cousin's in jail. So, he's looking for somebody to drive his limo. He'll pay five hundred bucks. You drive it down on Monday, do the Oscar thing and the parties afterwards, then drive it back on Tuesday.

"Fits your schedule like a glove. You wanna talk to my cousin?"

Johnny responds, "I dunno. Let me think about it."

CHAPTER FOUR

Swanky walks through an open-air mall and turns into the Malibu Cafe.

Roger, the suave maitre d', is happy to see her and addresses her with his charming French accent, "Good afternoon, Ms. Shampane."

As always, Swanky is thoroughly charmed. "Good afternoon, Roger. You're looking beautiful, as always."

Roger smiles and leads her over to a private table with an unobstructed view of the ocean. He pulls her chair out for her, "Is there anything I can do for you before your guest arrives?"

Swanky looks at him. "Roger, when you say, 'Is there anything you can do for me,' what is it that you actually mean?"

Roger enjoys this 'game,' which, apparently, he and Swanky have played before. Swanky continues, "Do you mean you are 'available' to bring me an appetizer?

"Or, are you suggesting that you would like to do something of a more sexual nature? In which case, you would be open to a sexual harassment lawsuit which could possibly cost you the fabulous Chez' Malibu Cafe."

Roger has a quick and nimble mind, "I most assuredly was intending the latter. Even though it might cost me the very restaurant that I've worked all my life to make one of the most prestigious in the world . . . I would gladly risk it just to share with you even a single moment of sexual eye contact."

They share a chuckle, and Swanky makes a slow assessment of his tall muscular physique. "Roger, Roger. Sometimes, I believe you are even more charming than me."

Roger smiles, nods, and leaves.

Swanky leans forward and inhales the fragrance from a vase of freshly cut flowers.

Soon thereafter, Roger leads Laura, Swanky's luncheon guest, to her table. Roger pulls her chair out for her, and she thanks him with a smile as she sits directly across from Swanky, "Nice job on the Vanity Fair interview."

Swanky nods. "Thanks. I've done better, I've done worse."

Laura looks up at Roger. "Roger, would you please bring us a bottle of your most semi-expensive wine. On my tab."

Roger smiles. "Please allow me to bring you a very special bottle of wine . . . compliments of the house."

Swanky reverts playfully back to the game, directing herself to Laura. "Didn't that sound rather sexual to you? The way he more or less suggested that I join him for a sleazy love tryst in his cozy little cottage down on the beach?"

Laura joins in the game. "Yes, it did."

Swanky guides the conversation. "I'm thinking of bringing a sexual harassment lawsuit against him for twelve million dollars."

Laura follows Swanky's lead, "Well, I definitely heard him sexually harass you, and I would gladly be your corroborating witness . . . partner."

All three share a laugh, and Roger leaves.

Laura smiles at Swanky. "I saw you on Conan's show last week. And I must say you've never sounded more sweet and wholesome."

Swanky nods. "You mean all that crap about growing up on a dairy farm in Wisconsin? That was Jimmy Hargrove's idea. He thinks it will make me seem less threatening, more like 'the girl next door.'

"I'm gonna get one of those lovable, mature-woman, romantic-comedy roles if it's the last thing I ever do."

Laura thinks back on this familiar name. "Jimmy Hargrove. I've often wondered if that man has ever worked a single day in his entire life. How does he do it? Seventy years of living without ever having a job."

Swanky smiles. "I told him the other night that he's the most brilliant man I've ever known. 'You wander from friend to friend for a month or two at a time, living rent-free in their guest house, close to the pool, and all that's required is that you bring along vast amounts of gossip and a nasty sense of humor.'"

Laura adds, "That would be a perfect job for me when I retire, except for that part about going from friend to friend. I can't stand being around my friends. But I do like that part about living rent-free in a guest house near the pool."

Roger returns with the wine, pours them each a glass, and they taste it. He then places the bottle next to the delicate vase containing a red rose. Swanky coos lecherously as he departs, "Thank you, Roger."

The conversation now turns to the reason behind this lunch date when Laura asks, "So, what's up?"

Swanky takes another sip. "Well, right at the moment, I'm just trying to get an accurate reading on Monday night. And who better to ask than my one and only friend, Hollywood's best rumor-analyzing commentator, Laura James."

Laura accepts this compliment with a nod, and offers her opinion on Monday night, "It looks like Nicholson again. He gave the best performance of the year in the best movie of the year, so–"

Swanky interrupts, "Why the hell would I care about Nicholson?"

Laura grins. "Oh, I must have misunderstood, I thought for one moment you were interested in someone other than yourself. I guess it's the Best Actress category you're interested in."

Swanky scoffs. "Follow the bouncing ball, Laura."

Laura responds, "It looks like Blaine."

Swanky fiddles with her silverware then slices roughly through a pad of butter. "Shit! Blaine. Again?"

"There's a pretty strong buzz in that direction."

"Blaine. What a bitch. They must think it takes a genius to do an accent. Hell, I did an accent in my first friggin' movie."

Laura chuckles. "You did a hillbilly accent in a French film."

"So what? It was an accent, wasn't it? That's just what she needs, another damn Oscar. You're my friend, Laura. Would you kill her for me?"

"Is it really that hard for you to accept?"

"Yes, actually."

"Why? You're still the highest-paid actress in the world."

Swanky clenches her teeth. "I want the OSCAR! And if I don't get it this year, I'll probably never have another chance at it.

"Everybody knows that my movie was just a cheap imitation of a high-grossing quality film. But nobody seems to realize that just because the movie was a piece of crap, doesn't mean that I wasn't great."

"Hasn't Universal helped push things along?"

"A few magazine covers, a few talk-shows, a few interviews, and that was it."

Laura interjects a little humor into the moment, "I did see the full-page ad in the *London Times* with you sitting backwards on a camel, wearing a bikini, lobbing hand grenades into Hitler's bunker."

"Shut up."

Laura smiles. "Well, at least you can say you were nominated."

Swanky hates that rationale. "I don't want to say I was nominated. Some day, I want to be able to say to my grandchildren . . . 'At the biggest and best Academy Awards ceremony . . . with the whole world watching . . . I kicked Victoria Blaine's ass.'"

Laura puts her head in her hands, laughing. "I think you've got to have children before you can have grandchildren."

Swanky is not amused. "When the time comes, I'll rent a couple of the little shits."

CHAPTER FIVE

In the visitor's room of the county jail, Fred and Johnny sit, looking through a thick glass window at Fred's cousin, Ralph, who appears rather unkempt but nevertheless quite authoritarian, as he evaluates the qualifications of the prospective driver of his limousine. "You vouching for this guy, Freddie?"

Fred nods. "Yeah, I'll vouch for him. I've worked with him for six years. I wouldn't bring him to you if I didn't trust him."

Ralph turns to Johnny. "Okay. Here's the deal. The limo is a little outdated and don't run quite so perfectly, so I'm sending a mechanic along with you. Her name is Lucy Lee."

Johnny raises his eyebrows. "She's a girl mechanic?"

Ralph cops an attitude. "Yes, 'she' is a girl mechanic. So, this afternoon the limo is having an Earl Scheib slapped on it. It don't run so great, but it'll look fantastic.

"Then, Monday morning, early, five o'clock, you leave Reno for L.A.

"First thing you do when you get there is have the limo washed and polished up nice and pretty. Then, you go directly to the Silver Stallion Limousine Service. A map in the glove box will show you how to get there. You'll talk to a guy named Bobby Rico. He'll tell you what to do.

"Then, on Tuesday, you drive back to Reno. Piece of cake.

"I'll give you five hundred bucks the day you get back. Also, you gotta wear a tuxedo. There's four of 'em in the trunk of the limo, all different sizes. One will fit you.

"Also, I've made a little change in the way the limo looks. So, if that butt-wipe Rico starts yelling about it, just tell him to 'shut the hell up,' because my contract don't say nuttin' about no sign on top of no roof. This is America. Every citizen has the right to advertise his stuff. It's in the constitution."

Ralph narrows his eyes and continues, "And whatever you do . . . don't let Lucy Lee drive. Got it?"

Johnny answers with vigor, "Got it."

Ralph stands to leave. "Thanks, Freddie. I owe ya." Ralph then cautions Johnny one last time, "Just remember what I said: Lucy Lee don't drive under no circumstances."

* * *

Johnny rides a bus on the outskirts of the city. The bus stops, and he gets out and walks down a dirt road leading to a trailer in the distance. As he approaches, a few chickens peck and cluck in a nearby pen.

He enters the trailer. One very old basset hound sleeps on the couch, and Johnny attempts to rough-house with the old hound but doesn't get much of a response, so he proceeds with what is obviously his daily routine of listening to his phone messages while fixing the hound's meal.

Johnny presses a button on his outdated answering machine, and today's lone message rewinds. He takes a can of dog food from the cupboard and clamps on an opener.

The message plays as Johnny slowly twists the can opener: "John, this is Rita. I called to ask a favor of you. Stewart and I are going to Myrna's Oscar party, and I would appreciate it if you didn't go. I'm just trying to avoid a scene. Stewart has a very quick temper, and he said he would take it as a personal insult if you were to show your face at Myrna's party."

The message clicks off. Johnny continues fixing the hound's meal.

CHAPTER SIX

Back at the craps table, Johnny is on break. Bob, Fred, and Monty, the current stickman, 'play with the money' as they wait for a game to get started.

Bob instigates a conversation, "So, I hear Rita's new lover-boy is telling people that he's gonna kick Johnny's ass if Johnny shows his face at Myrna's Oscar party."

Fred responds, "Don't worry, Johnny's not gonna be there. He's driving my cousin's limo to Hollywood."

Monty grins. "Wouldn't it be fabulous if he drove some star to the Oscars, and when the star stepped out of the limo, onto the red carpet, the television camera caught a glimpse of Johnny's face?"

All three burst a laugh at the thought of it.

Bob poses a logical question: "Have either of you guys ever wondered what Rita saw in him in the first place? They're the worst match I've ever seen. She's the life of the party . . . and he just wants to stand in the corner and observe things.

"Think about it. He's a hillbilly and she's a bitch . . . so what in the hell were they ever doing together in the first place. A bitch and a hillbilly aren't supposed to be together. A bitch and a bastard, yes. A hillbilly and another hillbilly, yes. But not a hillbilly and a bitch."

Monty chimes in, "You know what Johnny told me one time? It was a few years back, and we were standing on a dead game, shootin' the bull . . . talking about what we wanted out of life, and all that kind of shit . . . and Johnny said that all he wanted out of life was a woman who shared his enthusiasm for just being alive."

Monty shakes his head. "What kind of crazy goofball shit is that? Ricky Jones had the best philosophy . . . he said he would be perfectly content if he could have sex with fifteen different women every month for the rest of his life, plus a million bucks, plus never go bald."

Bob nods his head in agreement. "Ricky's always had his shit together!"

Fred moves on to a different topic. "You guys ever do an Oscar speech? You know what I mean? At home, in front of a mirror?"

Monty has a recollection, "I did an Oscar speech one night when I was driving home. It started at McCarran Boulevard, and it didn't finish until I rolled into my driveway.

"I must have thanked a hundred people. I couldn't stop. It was weird. It was like I was God announcing the names of the people I was gonna allow into Heaven.

"I even thanked the kid in first grade who found my Lone Ranger ring out on the playground and turned it in. Can you imagine that? A kid finds a Lone Ranger ring and turns it in. Unbelievable. And for being so honest . . . thirty years later, I put him in my Oscar speech."

Bob recalls his Oscar speech, "I had an Oscar speech 'dream' one time, and just as I got up to the podium and started to speak . . . I farted. It was the most horrible moment of my life."

Fred is horrified. "What'd you do?"

"I pretended like Tom Hanks did it."

Fred is hooked. "Then what happened?"

"Then the Oscar slipped out of my hands and fell on the floor."

Fred is stunned. "Oh man."

Bob continues, "And then, with my back to the audience, I bent over to pick it up, and the seat of my pants split apart, and I wasn't wearing underwear."

Fred recoils, "Geezuz!"

"And then I tried to back off the stage, but I stepped on my shoelace and fell over sideways. And then for some weird reason, my legs went into this spastic kicking fit, which caused me to lose control of my bowels."

Fred is appalled. "Holy crap!"

"And then everybody started screaming at me, and Madonna jumped up on stage and kicked me in the balls . . . and then I blacked out and Billy Bob Thornton dragged me away by the neck of my tuxedo jacket. It was the worst night of my life!"

Monty isn't impressed. "I had one kinda like that . . . I had this fabulous speech memorized, but when I got to the podium, I froze, and I couldn't remember anything, and I just kept saying, 'Aaah, aaah, aaah.' And then the music started up, and I walked off without having said one single word.

"And when I got back to my seat, my wife was crying because she was so ashamed of me. And because of that, my entire life took a nosedive. My wife divorced me, I became an alcoholic, a drug addict, and eventually . . . a dice dealer."

The three craps dealers burst a laugh at Monty's disregard for their vocation.

Fred tries to ad-lib his Oscar speech: "I'd just say that I owe it all to a little puppy named Skippy . . . who saved my life . . . when I was six years old . . . when he jumped in front of a locomotive . . . that had lost its brakes . . . and was hurtling . . . out of control . . . straight at me . . . but my foot was caught in a bear trap . . . and so Skippy–"

Monty's heard enough. "Shut up! Just . . . shut . . . up!"

Fred grumbles back, "It's as good as your stupid story."

Coming back from break, Johnny walks up to the craps table and moves into Monty's spot, Monty moves around the table into Fred's spot, Fred moves over to Bob's spot, and Bob goes on break.

Monty speaks to Johnny, "I hear you're gonna drive the stars around on Oscar night."

"Yep. I'm going to the Oscars."

Monty gets serious. "If you see Brad Pitt, tell him I need to talk to him. I've got a great idea for a movie."

Johnny smiles. "Yeah, okay."

Monty persists, "No, really. It's a story about this really good lookin' dice dealer who saves the world from terrorists. It's called . . . *The Monty Memoirs.*

"It's kind of a rags-to-riches story where this dealer goes from rags . . . to riches . . . I don't quite have the whole plot worked out . . . but . . . you know–"

Fred puts a halt to Monty's nonsense. "A little advice: therapy."

CHAPTER SEVEN

It's another perfect day in Malibu as Swanky lounges on a fabulous pool-side patio overlooking the ocean. She is deep in thought when the phone on the table next to her chaise lounge rings. She answers on speakerphone, "Hello."

Stanley responds, "It's me. I just want to go over this thing one more time. I'm not saying I can pull it off but just in case . . . you're saying that you would have no problem leaving that jerkoff Idors and coming back to CCA, is that correct?"

"That's right, Stanley, assuming, of course, that you quit giving those brainless, skinny-ass, no-talent, plastic-titted, smiley-faced mannequins the first look at any girl-next-door role that's worth half a shit. Why? You talk to Blaine? Is she willing to do it?"

"I haven't talked to anybody yet. I just wanted to first make sure we're clear on what the deal is."

"We're clear on the deal, Stanley, but that's not the problem. The problem is you've only got today and tomorrow to pull it together. Call me if you make it. Don't call me if you don't."

CHAPTER EIGHT

Back at the casino, twenty to thirty dealers have gathered at the bar for their after-shift drink. Fred, Monty, and Bob already have their drinks in hand.

Monty 'books' Oscar bets from his stool at the corner of the bar. "Anybody want Nicholson at even money? Nobody? At even money? Huh? Geezuz, gimme a break, who can beat the guy?"

Bob answers from several stools down the bar, "Four guys."

Monty acts surprised. "Like who?"

"Like DiCaprio. Like Nick Carlson. Like Denzel. Like Kevin Bacon."

Monty sees an opening, "Okay, you like Bacon? For half a mallard I'll give you even money on Bacon.

"Okay? Fifty bucks, and I'll throw in the Supporting Actress of your choice at three to one. Okay? You want it or were you just beating your gums?

"Or hey, how about this . . . Best Director. You pick, and I'll give you three to one."

Bob does the math. "Shouldn't that be four to one? There's five nominees. One's gonna win, four are gonna lose. That's four to one odds as I figure it. Freddie, am I right or wrong?"

Fred nods. "One winner, four losers. Sounds like a four to one shot to me."

Monty throws his hands in the air. "I'm giving you the pick for chrissake. I gotta get something for giving you the pick."

Bob replies, "Give me three-and-a-half to one, and I'll take Spielberg for a yard and a half."

Monty sneers. "Hey, Wall Street Bob, what do I look like, a friggin' idiot?"

Bob tries to sound reasonable, "C'mon, Spielberg's already won fifty fuckin' Oscars. They're not gonna give him another one."

"Okay, then you give me three-and-a-half to one and I'll take Spielberg."

Bob smiles. "Tell you what I will do. You give me forty to one, and I'll take Swanky Shampane for Best Actress."

Monty is stunned. "Forty to one?!"

Bob keeps a straight face. "Hey, everybody knows Blaine's a lock."

Monty mocks Bob's offer, "Blaine's a lock?"

"That's right."

Monty calls his bluff. "Okay, just to show you how the balls of a real dice dealer work, I'm gonna give you that forty to one. How much you in for?"

Bob quickly fires back. "How 'bout a hundred?! How 'bout two hundred?!"

Monty pushes it. "C'mon! Bring it! I'll take every cent you've got!"

Johnny walks up with a beer and joins the crowd, giving Bob and Monty each 'a way out.'

Fred looks at Johnny, "So, you all set for tomorrow?"

Johnny smiles. "Yep. Hope I get to drive Victoria Blaine."

Monty pounces. "Yeah, you'll probably drive Victoria. She probably doesn't have her own driver. And she's probably just dying to be chauffeured to the Academy Awards by some dice-dealing chicken farmer."

Laughter erupts all around them.

Fred gets things back on track. "I'm gonna drop the limo off at your trailer tonight. I'll draw you a map on how to get to Lucy Lee's place, and leave it on the front seat with the keys. What time are you leaving in the morning?"

Johnny thinks about it. "Early. About four o'clock. I want to give us enough time for a nice leisurely drive down."

Fred nods. "Good. And my cousin said don't forget to have the limo polished up nice and pretty once you get there.

"And he also wanted me to remind you . . . don't let Lucy Lee drive, no matter what."

* * *

It's four in the morning. The desert is dark and quiet. Johnny steps out of his trailer carrying a script, sees the limo, smiles, gets in, and drives off to pick up Lucy Lee.

With that new paint job, the limo sure looks fabulous . . . aside from the large banana-shaped 'survival yellow' sign strapped to its roof, advertising: "POTATO-BUTT JOHNSON PLUMBING – 'Call me when your bowels are moving but your pipes ain't.'"

* * *

High up in the mountains, at the Mt. Rose Ski Resort, surrounded by huge pine trees and deep snow, overlooking Lake Tahoe, is an 'employees housing area.' Lucy Lee, a Chinese girl between thirty and forty, sits on a high snowbank, waiting. The cold black sky is thick with twinkling stars.

The limo pulls into the parking lot and rolls to a stop near a parked snowplow.

With a first-aid fanny pack around her waist, Lucy Lee slides off the snowbank and, carrying one old suitcase and a small tool kit, walks over to introduce herself.

Johnny pops the trunk latch and steps out to meet her. The engine is left running.

"Hi, I'm Johnny Johnson. You must be Lucy Lee."

Lucy shakes Johnny's hand. "Nice to meet you."

Johnny reciprocates, "Nice to meet you." And, indicating to the surroundings, asks, "You live here?"

Lucy Lee answers, "I live here and I work here. I'm a ski instructor."

Johnny smiles. "Nice." He then reaches out to take her suitcase. "I'll put your suitcase in the trunk and we'll be off."

Lucy Lee holds onto her bag. "You go ahead and get in the car. I'll put my suitcase into the trunk. It's unlucky to let someone carry your luggage."

Johnny smiles. "Okay, you're the boss."

Lucy Lee smiles. "No. You're the boss.'

Johnny nods. "Okay. I'm the boss."

She smiles and corrects him. "You're the boss of you, and I'm the boss of me."

Sounds good to Johnny. "Okay."

After Lucy Lee places her suitcase into the trunk, struggling to position it 'just so,' and as Johnny reaches in to improve its position by moving the tuxedos out of the way, Lucy Lee inadvertently slams the trunk lid down on his fingers.

Johnny shrieks as the lid bounces back open.

Lucy Lee is mortified by what she has done, but being a person always ready to rectify problems, she promptly wrestles Johnny to the ground. "I'm sorry! I'm sorry! Your fingers are dented, I need to splint them!"

Johnny, writhing in pain, is too preoccupied to argue.

Holding him down with her knee on his stomach, Lucy Lee

then opens her fanny pack and extracts finger splints, gauze, and a roll of tape. Then proceeds to wrap his fingers.

Whimpering as he suffers, Johnny courteously allows Lucy Lee to finish the process, even though the black exhaust from the limo is spewing directly into his face, causing him to sneeze and cough.

Completing her paramedical duties, Lucy Lee suddenly notices the problem from the limo's exhaust pipe and jumps up to rectify it.

She darts to the driver-side door, yanks it open, jumps in, yanks the shift-lever into gear, and the limo instantly lurches into motion. Unfortunately, Lucy Lee has shifted into reverse, and thus run the limo over Johnny's legs.

Fortunately, the limo is brought to an abrupt halt by impacting with the nearby snowplow, allowing the panic-stricken Lucy Lee to jump out and dash back for further doctoring of the terrorized victim. "I'm sorry! I'm sorry! Your legs are dented! I need to splint them!"

Johnny is wild-eyed with fear. "No! No! You missed! I'm fine! I'm fine!"

* * *

Lucy Lee's feelings are hurt. But they drive down Highway 395, advancing through the Nevada desert, without mentioning their recent fiasco.

Finally, without looking at Johnny, Lucy Lee breaks the silence. "Are you mad at me?"

Wanting to be accurate, Johnny thinks carefully before answering. "I'm afraid of you."

CHAPTER NINE

Beverly Hills in the morning.

Swanky enters a stylish building on Wilshire Blvd and, walking past the reception-security desk, gives a slight nod without slowing down before entering the elevator.

The elevator doors open, Swanky exits, brushes past the outer secretary. The inner secretary then momentarily considers an attempt to stop her, but by then Swanky has pushed open a large, black marble door that features gold-block lettering: "IDORS INTERNATIONAL MANAGEMENT."

Michael Idors, in his late fifties, exuding power and panache, sits at a large desk, talking on the phone. The decor is extraordinarily plush. Swanky takes a seat straight across from him and indicates with her fingers for him to wrap up his call.

Idors does as directed. "Marty, let me call you back." He

then smiles at Swanky. "If I'd known you were coming, I'd have worn my new tie."

Swanky ignores his good humor. "Do you know where I'm seated tonight?"

Idors answers, "Well, I would expect you're seated where the Best Actress nominees are always seated . . . within the first five rows, near an aisle."

Swanky's attitude has already made clear that her presence is not to be misinterpreted as a social visit. "Do you consider six seats in . . . near an aisle?"

Idors attempts to deflect what seems to be developing. "Not exactly on the aisle, but still . . . a pretty good seat."

Swanky is not having it. "If you think that's a pretty good seat, what would you call front row, center seat?"

Now he understands. "I'd call that the best seat in the house."

Swanky won't be diverted. "I'd call it Victoria Blaine's seat."

Idors exhales. "Ahh, the Blaine thing."

Swanky clarifies the precise reason for her being there. "Get me the seat next to her."

Idors laughs. "I can't do that. That's her husband's seat."

Swanky responds, "The other side. Where Nicholson's sitting."

"I can't do that. Who do you think I am . . . the dictator of Hollywood?"

Swanky scowls. "Use your juice. Stanley could do it."

Her last remark crossed the line. "Bullshit. That prick couldn't juice Streisand into a karaoke bar."

Swanky gets up from her chair and heads for the door. "I'll wait until noon before I ask him. Gimme a call."

CHAPTER TEN

Johnny and Lucy Lee drive along without conversation. Highway 395 is a lonely road, with very little traffic and very few markets or gasoline stations along the way. And so it was when they heard the first knock of the engine.

Lucy Lee asks, "Did you hear that?"

The last thing Johnny wants to hear is that they have a mechanical problem. "No. I didn't hear anything."

Lucy Lee is prepared for all problems, at all times. "That noise."

Johnny is still hoping to avoid any trouble, at least until he has regained the full use of his fingers and legs. "Probably just something not serious."

But Lucy Lee has a keen ear for automotive troubleshooting. "I can't be sure, but I think you have a knock in your muffler."

Johnny is not familiar with that particular problem. "A knock in the muffler? I don't believe I've ever heard of that."

Lucy Lee knows what to do. "Better pull over so I can take a look."

Johnny slows the limo to a stop on the shoulder of the road. Lucy Lee gets out, tool kit in hand.

She stands behind the limo with one hand on her hip as she thinks. Johnny gets out and, hobbling from his leg injuries, joins her at the back of the limo where he will await her evaluation of the situation. The tail light that impacted the snowplow has a large chunk of red plastic busted out of it, and he notices.

Lucy Lee issues a preliminary location of the trouble: "The muffler is connected to the carbinator, right?

Johnny shrugs. "I've never owned a car. I know absolutely nothing about how they work."

Lucy Lee bends down to crawl under the vehicle. "Okay. Stand back. I'm going to adjust the muffler belts."

Once Lucy Lee is under the limo and out of sight, noises are heard, suggesting that mechanical things are being accomplished.

And before long, Lucy Lee crawls back into the sunlight, dragging along her tool kit. She dusts herself off and, smiling, gives Johnny a thumbs-up.

Johnny returns the thumbs-up, and they get back into the limo. Lucy Lee seems pleased. And Johnny inquires about her skillful achievement, "Belts too loose?"

Lucy Lee politely corrects him, "Bolts, too tight."

Johnny nods and turns on the ignition.

The limo instantly blasts a frightening noise as the entire muffler system shoots out its rear end.

Johnny looks at Lucy Lee. She nods expertly. "We shouldn't have any more trouble with that darn thing."

With the automotive problem now behind them, Lucy notices the script on the dashboard and picks it up. "What's this?"

Johnny smiles with the pride of ownership. "Just a script I wrote."

"What's it about?"

"How to save the world."

Lucy Lee beams with the pride of knowing a writer with such humanitarian sensibilities. "What are you going to do with it?"

Like any writer, Johnny is always willing to talk about his lofty literary ambitions. "Give it to Steven Spielberg . . . if I ever see him. Would you just set it on the back seat for safekeeping?"

Lucy Lee nods, and flips it over her shoulder, through the separation window, and into the back seat. Johnny sighs. "Thanks."

CHAPTER ELEVEN

Swanky enters Chateau du Baptiste, a private boutique in the heart of Beverly Hills.

It's morning. Monsieur Baptiste and his staff are making last-minute adjustments for tonight's 'red carpet' dresses.

Swanky has put on a stunning black, long-sleeved, low-cut dress. Monsieur Baptiste pins out a few minor wrinkles as he schmoozes with his exquisite French accent. "I have never seen a dress look more beautiful."

Swanky teases him. "Beautiful or gorgeous?"

Baptiste plays this game better than anyone. "Absolutely, gorgeous."

Swanky toys with him. "Gorgeous or dazzling?"

Baptiste purrs with emotional hand gestures. "Gorgeously dazzling, in an elegant, yet most erotic way."

Swanky adds a revealing subtext to her essence, "Do you

think the average guy watching the Oscars would give up all his worldly possessions to have sex with the woman who wears this dress?"

Baptiste applies the perfect blend of humor to the moment, "I would give a million dollars just to gargle from a single cup of her bathwater."

Swanky chuckles. "Baptiste, do I owe you money?"

"Oui. I believe Mademoiselle has yet to pay for her Golden Globe dress."

Swanky has an answer already prepared. "Oh yes, the dress I wore, which looked pathetically similar to Victoria Blane's dress."

Baptiste coughs uncomfortably.

Swanky extracts what she needs to be an absolute certainty. "I expect that isn't going to happen tonight."

Baptiste finishes the pinning and unzips the dress so that Swanky can step out of it. "No, no, that will not happen tonight. I can absolutely guarantee you of that." Swanky steps behind a dressing screen and Baptiste continues the conversation, "You are wearing a low-cut black satin, and Madame Blaine is wearing a high-necked white silk. Two very different styles."

Baptiste addresses his assistant, "Once Mademoiselle's dress is sewn and pressed, have it delivered before all others."

He then turns back to Swanky. "Your dress will be at your home by no later than two o'clock."

Swanky smiles. "Thank you, Baptiste."

Baptiste speaks sincerely before turning away to walk back through the curtains into the pressing room. "Good luck tonight, Mademoiselle."

"Thank you, Baptiste."

Finished dressing, Swanky emerges from behind the screen and, on her way out of the building, notices a clothing bar holding a plastic, see-through bag . . . enclosing a high-necked white silk dress. She pauses to have a closer look.

There is a deep sadness in the way Swanky unzips the bag a few inches and touches the dress before leaving.

CHAPTER TWELVE

The limousine travels through the desert of Highway 395 without further complications, though rather loudly.

Johnny's leg injuries are still painful, but it's his splintered fingers that seem to bother him the most as they snack on Fritos and prunes.

However, Johnny is not one to hold grudges, and they converse without alluding to the inconvenience of his constant squirming around trying to get comfortable. "So, where are you from Lucy? Should I call you Lucy, or Lucy Lee?"

Lucy Lee smiles. "I was named after Lucille Ball and Louie Lee."

"Who's Louie Lee?"

"My father says Louie Lee was the luckiest person in the world."

Johnny is curious. "Really. I don't think I've ever heard of him."

"He was a multi-millionaire. But he was a pretty stingy guy from what I've heard. He's dead now. He died the morning I was born. My father said his spirit of luckiness entered my body that morning. And so that's how my middle name came to be Lee."

"Lee is your middle name?"

"Yes. It is also my family name."

"So, Lee is your last name and your middle name?"

"Yes."

"So your whole name is Lucy Lee Lee?"

"Yes."

Johnny nods and turns his eyes back to the highway where he can watch the road and have a quiet moment to himself.

After a number of aborted thoughts that appeared to cause his lips to move, Johnny is still in need of information. "Was Louie Lee also a member of your family?"

"Yes. Louie Lee was my father's twin brother."

Johnny nods and turns his attention back to the road.

And again, there are facial tics and silent thoughts before Johnny feels compelled to get more of the story. "What did Louie Lee die of?"

"Forgetfulness."

Johnny nods and waits patiently for the rest of the story.

"He was a skydiver, and on the morning of his last jump, when he died, he forgot to put on his parachute."

Johnny is now even more curious. "And yet your father thought he was the luckiest guy in the world?"

"That wasn't the first time he'd forgotten."

Again, there is an understanding nod. Then Johnny turns his attention back to the road and his private, yet animated thoughts.

CHAPTER THIRTEEN

As the morning in Beverly Hills buzzed with conversations related to tonight's Oscar activities, Swanky had one more stop to make before she could return home and relax by the pool.

She walks past two security guards and enters the luxurious surroundings of intimate coves and nooks where the world's finest jewelry is displayed by invitation only. She is immediately led into a private parlor where two gray suede chairs face each other across an elaborately engraved, sterling-silver coffee table, inlaid with a layer of precious stones. A diamond-encrusted hand mirror lays on a black velvet cushion atop the table.

The room's attendant smiles and speaks before leaving, "I'll tell Mr. Winston you're here."

Swanky only waits a few seconds before an elderly, silver-haired gentleman carrying a thick gold and leather case enters. He approaches Swanky and they embrace warmly.

They sit and Mr. Winston smiles as he places the case on the table. "I'm ready if you are."

Swanky nods and Mr. Winston unlocks the case and describes its contents before revealing them. "The tear-drop earrings feature two emeralds taken from the Muzo mine in Bogota, Colombia in 1797. They are mounted in platinum, and set off by sixteen perfectly cut diamonds from the Golconda mines of India.

"They once belonged to Princess Diana and were auctioned just this past October in London where they sold for sixteen million eight-hundred and seventy-five thousand dollars."

Mr. Winston now takes the earrings out of the case and hands them over one at a time for Swanky to try on.

With the gems dangling from her ears, Swanky picks up the hand mirror to admire them. "I didn't know my ears could be so ravishing."

Mr. Winston expands his smile. "And, for another thirteen-point-seven million . . . the matching necklace. A piece inspired by the original setting of the Jonker emerald."

Mr. Winston lifts the necklace from the case, stands, and places it lovingly around Swanky's neck.

She breathes deeply as her hand angles the mirror from side to side. "Oh, Harry."

After taking her time to admire it from numerous angles, Swanky takes it off and hands it, and the earrings, back to Mr. Winston.

Swanky feigns a pout. "If I don't win tonight, may I keep them as a consolation prize?"

Mr. Winston smiles and places the items back inside the case. "I'm afraid these would be woefully inadequate to counterbalance the outrageous injustice of your not winning . . . hence, I would never allow them to be, in any way, a part of some presumptuous notion that mere trinkets such as these could ever compensate you for . . . such a criminal act by the Academy."

Swanky chuckles through a smile. "You're good, Harry."

Mr. Winston nods. "I practice at home."

CHAPTER FOURTEEN

Johnny and Lucy Lee drive along with The Captain and Tennille singing "Rocky Raccoon" on the radio. A cafe is just ahead, and Johnny looks at his watch. "It's almost eleven o'clock. Maybe we ought to stop for lunch."

Johnny indicates to the small cafe with the large sign above it reading: "WANDA'S–THE WORLD'S FRIENDLIEST CAFE." "You hungry?"

Lucy nods. "I am very hungry."

The limo turns off towards the wide spot in the road where the cafe is situated. Johnny is also very hungry. "And how about this for luck . . . we'll be eating at the world's friendliest cafe."

Johnny noses the limo up to the cafe as Lucy Lee gives him a little advice, "Johnny, you shouldn't say that."

Johnny is puzzled. "Say what?"

Lucy Lee cautions him. "You know."

Johnny makes an honest but unsuccessful effort to figure out what she is referring to. "I don't think I know."

Lucy Lee tells him, "Johnny, you should not speak about good luck before it happens."

"Why not?"

"Because that turns your good luck into bad luck."

Johnny turns the engine off and smiles. "No offense, Lucy Lee, but I don't believe in that kind of stuff."

Lucy Lee smiles back and opens her door. Johnny opens his, and they exit the limo.

The cafe door is ajar and they enter.

There is one small, square table with one chair on each side. On the table is a bell with a card leaned against it that reads: RING BELL FOR SERVICE. A shotgun and a moose's head are on display over the front window.

Johnny pulls out a chair for Lucy Lee.

Lucy Lee smiles, walks around to the other side of the table, and pulls out a chair for Johnny.

They smile at each other.

Then, they both walk halfway around the table and sit in the chairs that were pulled out for them.

Johnny rings the bell.

Before long, a very old lady shuffles slowly through the swinging doors leading from the kitchen, wearing a checkered apron with a matching hair cover. She takes an order pad from her apron and a pencil from behind her ear as she approaches the table. "Good morning. Welcome to Wanda's, the world's friendliest cafe. May I take your order?"

Lucy Lee and Johnny smile and greet their waitress, "Good morning."

They both appear to like old people. "May we see your menu, please?"

The waitress pulls a plastic, single-sided menu from her apron and sets it on the table between them.

Because there is only one menu between the two people sitting opposite each other, getting the thing read is a somewhat clumsy process. And so begins the back-and-forth movement of the menu, which seems to be based on a politeness bordering somewhat close to certifiable stupidity.

After waiting beyond a reasonable amount of time for the menu to be read, the waitress comments, "Take your time."

Lucy Lee and Johnny smile then get back to their menu, with Johnny pointing out that the five ninety-nine breakfast includes toast and coffee.

Thinking aloud, Lucy Lee considers another possibility. "I might just have a muffin and orange juice."

More time passes as the menu continues to be studied.

The waitress comments again, "I'm eighty-seven years old."

Again, Lucy Lee and Johnny look up at her and smile, and Johnny is compelled by the time-honored and well-intentioned tradition of 'flirting with the old person.' "Get outta here, you're not eighty-seven. You don't look a day over twenty-seven."

(In fact, she looks like a hundred and eighty-seven.)

The waitress leans on the table and remarks, "I'd like to get your order before I turn eighty-eight."

Lucy Lee and Johnny exchange smiles: 'senior citizens can be absolutely adorable.'

Johnny is soon ready to order. "I guess I'll have the number three . . . 'Wanda's special farmhouse omelet.'"

The waitress writes down Johnny's order, and turns to Lucy Lee, who is just making her decision. "I believe . . . I will have . . . theeee . . . Belgian waffles . . . with . . . theeee . . . fresh strawberry syrup. And just the tiniest little strip of Canadian bacon."

The waitress writes down Lucy Lee's order, puts the order pad back in her apron, puts the pencil back behind her ear, and heads back to the kitchen. But after only two or three slow steps, Johnny adds to his order, "And could I have a cup of coffee, please?"

The waitress returns to the table, pulls her order pad back out of her apron, pulls her pencil back out from behind her ear, and adds the word "coffee" to Johnny's order. She then looks over to Lucy Lee.

Lucy Lee considers for a moment, then makes another decision, "I believe . . . I will also have . . . theeee . . . orange juice."

The waitress writes that down, then asks, with an attitude somewhat short of being overly friendly, "Anything else?"

Lucy Lee looks at Johnny. Johnny looks at the waitress, adding a little chuckle for friendliness' sake. "I guess that'll do us."

The waitress puts the pencil back behind her ear, the order pad back into her apron, and begins her slow trek back to the kitchen.

But apparently, Lucy Lee does have an additional request, "I almost forgot, would you be sure to use Egg Beaters in my friend's omelet."

Now, as Lucy Lee explains to Johnny that he has to be more careful about his cholesterol intake, the waitress turns back around, pulls out her order pad and her pencil, makes the "Egg Beaters" notation, and asks, "Anything else?"

Johnny shakes his head and politely mouths the words "no thank you."

Lucy Lee considers the question, then asks, "Has your orange juice got pulp in it?"

An immediate pall settles on the scene.

The waitress then undertakes the slow process of making her way over to the front window, where she can then climb up onto a small stool, reach the shotgun, take it down, load it with the two cartridges that she carries in her bra, aim, and fire.

This slowly developing endeavor has Lucy Lee and Johnny's utmost attention and curiosity. And they seem increasingly puzzled by their waitress' odd behavior as she narrates a personal story while moving along, "One time, when I was just a little girl about ten years old, I was up in an apple tree, and I saw a man driving the first automobile I had ever seen.

"He came down a bumpy dirt road, stopped at our family's farm, got out of the automobile, took a drink of whisky, climbed through a barbed-wire fence, walked a hundred yards across a soggy pasture . . . and peed on our cow.

"And I can remember thinking to myself at the time . . . *Should I just let it go? Or should I get my daddy's shotgun and kill him?*

"I let it go. And I've always regretted that decision. I've often wished that I'd blown his fuckin' head off."

Things have now advanced to where the waitress has climbed up onto the stool, taken down the shotgun, gotten back down from the stool, pulled out the two cartridges, and is currently loading the moose-killing shotgun.

At this point, Lucy Lee and Johnny exchange meaningful eye contact as the waitress continues her story, "My kids used to say that it was a real shame that someday I would probably freak out . . . all because somebody from the city peed on our cow."

Lucy Lee and Johnny get out of their chairs and proceed in a dignified, though rapid, exit, as the waitress continues, "But to tell you the truth . . . I've been kinda looking forward to it."

Lucy Lee and Johnny have left the cafe and are fast-walking to the limo.

The shotgun is now loaded and ready to shoot as the waitress heads for the door in hot, but slow, pursuit.

Lucy Lee and Johnny jump into the limo. The engine starts.

The waitress reaches the front door, raises the shotgun, and aims.

The limo spits up dirt as it tears away.

The waitress fires a blast and the lid of the limo's trunk bursts open, twisting violently upward against the back window.

The waitress fires again, and one of the limo's side-view mirrors is instantly blown apart and left dangling by a wire.

The two passengers duck their heads as they speed off down the road.

Once out of danger, they look at each other. Johnny seems a bit confused. "What the heck was that all about?"

Lucy Lee has a logical explanation. "I guess she's still pretty mad about the cow incident, and we just happened to be handy when she remembered it, and so she took it out on us. That's my guess."

Johnny can go along with that logic. "Yeah, that's what I was thinking."

Lucy Lee suddenly notices blood on Johnny's ear. "Johnny, you've been hit!"

"Am I hit bad?!!!"

Lucy Lee quickly examines his ear. "No! It's only a flesh wound! But I still have to splint it!"

Lucy Lee grabs her tool kit, extracts the splints, gauze, and tape, and, speaking as she goes, reaches for Johnny's ear, "Geez, it missed me completely. I must be luckier than heck."

CHAPTER FIFTEEN

Back home after her last stop in Beverly Hills, Swanky sits on the couch watching a pre-Oscar entertainment show on television. The splendor of the Pacific Ocean is in full view through the great expanse of windows half-circling this magnificent structure of weathered beams and rock.

On a large television screen, male and female hosts sit in director's chairs talking about tonight's Academy Awards. A soft buzz comes from an intercom built into the fireplace rocks. Swanky answers, "Hello."

A female voice responds, "It's me."

Swanky presses a button that unlocks a door and Sandra, a woman in he late thirties, enters the living room carrying a manicurist's kit and a stainless steel fold-up tray.

Swanky greets her, "Good morning, Sandra."

Sandra replies, "Good morning. And my, my, my . . . how calm you look."

Swanky smiles at her, and Sandra proceeds to set up for the manicure. "I would be a jittery nerve end if I were you. Just the thought of standing in front of a billion people . . . and then, on top of that, having to open my mouth and say something. I swear to you I couldn't do it. I get panicky just thinking about it."

Swanky grins. "Well, I probably would be a little panicky myself if I had at least a whore's chance in heaven of winning, but since I don't, I won't be having to say anything. So, nothing to get panicky about. I might even have a couple drinks before I get there."

Sandra bursts a laugh, and Swanky immediately joins her as she too enjoys how ridiculous her last comment had sounded.

Sandra adds to the silliness, "Yeah, what the heck, it's the greatest night of your life . . . enjoy it. Have a couple drinks in the limo on your way there, and then . . . when you get there . . . have a couple more."

Sandra is on a roll and continues through their laughter, "Yeah, let your hair down, have a ball . . . get sloppy."

Sandra has an infectious way of laughing as she speaks, and Swanky is anxious to keep the fun going. "Maybe I ought to do some drugs while I'm at it."

Sandra doesn't miss a beat. "Yeah! Quaaludes!"

Swanky is loving this 'tempting of the devil.' "Yeah! And

then, when they introduce the Best Actress nominees, and the camera comes in for a close shot of me . . . I could be snoring in my sleep! Honking like a duck!"

The visual image of Swanky's last remark throws them both into hysterics. And Sandra manages to add to the vision, "That would be perfect! And maybe, if you 'threw up' beforehand . . . you might still have some of the barf stuck to your dress!"

Swanky encourages the 'nightmare,' "Yeah!"

"And maybe a clump in your hair!"

"Yeah!"

Sandra is laughing so hard she can barely keep up, "And maybe when you were barfing . . . some snot drizzled out of your nose . . . and while you're snoring in your drunken slumber with billions of people watching . . . the snot would bubble in and out of your nostrils."

The horror of this absurdity propels them into wild howls of insane laughter.

Finally, Swanky regains control, sighs deeply, and speaks as she moves to sit on a stool at the bar. "Oh yeah! That would be some kind of fun."

Eventually, things wind down enough for Sandra to start setting up her equipment. "It's kind of scary where the mind chooses to go sometimes."

"Yes, it is. But in fact . . . that's the kind of Oscar night that actually haunts me."

Sandra lays out her tools. "You're kidding."

"No, I'm not. Because I know that I am, at all times, especially stressful times . . . just one quick little bad decision away from having a night like that.

"Believe me, I've already had one in my lifetime, so I know how easily they can get started."

Swanky moves to a chair near the window. Sandra sits opposite her. The manicuring tools are on a white towel on the table between them.

Sandra is curious about that night Swanky alluded to. "Wanna talk about it?"

"No. Not really. It was a long time ago, when my name was still Alice Johnson. But I'm over it. I have no need to talk about it."

Sandra is now even more curious. "Please."

"No."

"Please."

"No."

"If you tell me about it, then I promise I'll tell you immediately . . . the next time I hear some really disgusting gossip."

Swanky docsn't hesitate. "I mooned the principal of Ulysses S. Grant High School in Virginia City, Nevada . . . from the stage . . . on graduation night . . . in front of my friends, my friends' parents, my teachers, five or six of my foster parents, several of my probation officers, many personal enemies, and another couple hundred people I didn't even know.

"And I did this because the guy I was hanging around with

at the time said it would be the greatest thing that anybody could ever do . . . but that nobody in our class would ever have the balls to do it."

Sandra, with a smile ready to break into a laugh, just looks at her. "You're not gonna believe this, but I thought about doing that same thing myself.

"Actually, my cousin was gonna do it, but he chickened out. But when he first told me that he was thinking about doing it . . . I told him that if he did it, I'd do it.

"Thank God he chickened out."

Swanky grins. "Would you have done it, if he'd done it?"

"Heck no. My parents would have dropped over deader than a doornail."

Again they laugh together as Swanky blows on her nails.

The phone rings. Swanky asks, "Would you get that, and just put us on speakerphone?"

Sandra does as requested, and Swanky speaks towards speakerphone, "Hello."

Stanley's voice has its usual air of self-assurance, "Hello Swanky. I'm calling to tell you that three of the nominees said they would not even consider mentioning you in their Oscar speech. I didn't bother calling Blaine."

"Well, you did about as good as I expected. Goodbye."

Before Sandra can stand back up to press the phone off, Stanley has a little more to say, "However, I did find somebody who was willing to mention you."

"Who?"

"Cecil Clay."

Swanky is not overwhelmed by this news. "Who the hell is Cecil Clay?"

"Cinematographer on *The Road to Jack's House*, probably gonna win. It's between him and the guy who did *King Boss*.

"He said he'd be willing to say something like . . . he's thankful for the Academy's recognition of his work and that now maybe somebody will trust him enough to let him shoot a movie with . . . quote, unquote . . . 'Blaine or Shampane.'" There is a momentary pause before Stanley continues, "But he doesn't come cheap. He wants to associate-produce your next movie."

Swanky considers the offer. "Where are you now?"

"I'm at the agency. I'll be here until three o'clock."

"I'll get back to you within the hour."

"And Swanky . . . my end stays the same . . . you leave Idors and come back to CCA on a long-term contract."

"I'll call you within the hour."

"All right, but don't bother calling unless you accept the entire deal as I just laid it out."

The phone on Stanley's end clicks off, leaving Swanky's speakerphone buzzing.

Sandra attends to it.

Swanky returns her attention to the manicure, speaking with the kind of irony that she and Sandra seem to enjoy so much, "What kind of degenerate world are we living in when a fuckin' cinematographer thinks he can play hardball with a star.

"Nobody has any respect for the rules anymore. It's gotten so unfair. There was a time, not that many years ago, when I could have ruined that man's entire career with a simple phone call, but now . . ."

As Swanky's voice trails off, Sandra smiles and takes her cue, "It just doesn't seem right that such an unethical, egotistical, money-grubbing, low-life weasel could even be considered for an Oscar."

With a straight face, Swanky looks at Sandra. "Did you mean him, or me?"

This remark sends them both into uncontrollable convulsions of laughter.

An elderly gentleman, Jimmy Hargrove, tan and stylish, walks into view through a window overlooking the pool area. He enters the house. "Good morning, everyone." He then approaches Sandra. "I don't believe I've had the pleasure."

Swanky introduces them, "Jimmy, this is Sandra Wilson, quite possibly the world's greatest manicurist. Sandra, this is Jimmy Hargrove, quite possibly the world's greatest loafer."

Jimmy laughs and shakes Sandra's hand, then turns to Swanky. "Swanky, darling, I hate to be a complainer, but those hideous curtains in the guest house allow in a most unsettling glare from the pool. I've been awake since almost ten o'clock."

Swanky commiserates, "You poor thing. Maybe I should sell this dump and find a place without a pool-glare."

Jimmy saunters over to the bar and fixes himself a Bloody Mary, conversing during the process, "I'd hate to have you go to all that trouble just for me. A set of very dark curtains should suffice quite nicely."

He then takes an egg from the small bar refrigerator, cracks it into his drink, and heads back to his guest quarters after first making a polite exit.

"It was very nice meeting you, Sandra." He then turns to Swanky. "I'll be out at my office trying desperately to catch up on my sleep."

Swanky lampoons him with empathy. "Try with all your might, Jimmy. Just say to yourself, 'I can do it, I can do it.'"

Jimmy plays along, "I'll give it my best. That's all a person can do."

Swanky gives him a thumbs-up.

CHAPTER SIXTEEN

At the Dolby Theater, with security all over the place, things are in the midst of the last rehearsal for tonight's Academy Awards show.

Posters with the nominees' pictures on them are spread throughout the first ten rows of seats. Brian Gates, the director, is in a no-nonsense mood as someone has apparently missed his cue, again.

Brian, speaking through a headset, communicates with his technical staff manning the monitors up in the control room, "Damn it to hell! For the last time . . . I want the smoke to shoot in immediately after the first two bars. Not three bars, not two-and-a-half bars . . . two, bars.

"We've been rehearsing this thing for two days. What does it take to push a button on cue? Try it again."

At this point, the dancers line up to try it again, and just as the music starts up, one of the assistant directors approaches Brian with a phone. "Brian, I hate to bother you right at the moment, but you have a call on line two."

Brian can't believe it. "A call? Now? Are you crazy?"

"I think it might be important."

"I don't give a shit who it is or what it's about. Have somebody else deal with it."

Brian dismisses the assistant director by turning away from him. But the assistant director persists, "It's Michael Idors."

The name gets Brian's attention. He sighs deeply, takes the phone, and presses the button for line two.

"Hey, Mike, what's up?"

Idors is at his agency, at his desk, on a speakerphone. "Hi Brian, you know I wouldn't call you at a time like this if it weren't important. But I've got a little problem."

"How can I help you, Mike?"

"First, let me say I just got off the phone with ICM. They just made a vacancy in their mailroom. Your son can start tomorrow morning."

"That's great, Mike. Bernie graduated summa cum laude from Harvard last fall. He's eager, and he's a very tough kid. He can handle it."

"I'll be rooting for him. And the other reason I called is because I need to have Swanky Shampane sitting up front tonight, in Nicholson's seat."

"Oh Mike, I can't do that. You know I can't do that."

"I just talked to Jack, and he said he doesn't give a shit where he sits as long as he can get to the bar and back without a lot of hassle. I was thinking you could move Kevin Bacon over to Shampane's seat and put Jack there on the aisle."

"Bacon would never go for that."

"I'm giving Bacon's wife a chance to direct a little independent film in the fall. I just told her about it a few minutes ago. She told me Kevin will have no problem being off the aisle. So, everything is tits if you're okay with it."

Brian chuckles. "Yeah, what the hell."

"All right then, Brian, I owe you. Gimme a call whenever you need me."

"Thanks, Mike."

"Thank you, Brian." Idors hangs up.

* * *

Back in Malibu, Sandra has just finished Swanky's nails. The phone rings, Swanky presses the speaker button with her knuckle, then lounges back into the couch. "Hello."

"Hello Swanky," Michael Idors answers. "How are you doing, getting a little nervous about tonight?"

"That all depends on where I'm sitting."

"Would you be nervous if you were sitting front row center seat?"

64

"Oh Michael, you're kidding! Don't kid Michael. It's not nice!"

"Why would I kid you? Isn't this kind of why you left Mr. Numbnuts to go with me?"

"You're wonderful! You're the best!"

"I gotta go. Good luck tonight."

Before he can get off the line, Swanky asks another favor. "Michael, there's a guy, Cecil Clay, cinematographer on *The Road to Jack's House*, probably gonna get an Oscar tonight. He'll mention my name in his Oscar speech if he can associate-produce my next movie. Will you arrange it for me?"

"I already got Stanley to do the leg work."

"Geezuz, Swanky."

"Michael, please. Please."

"You expect me to break into CCA and grab a cinematographer that they have kept working at a very substantial salary for ten or fifteen years?"

"It doesn't matter. He'll deal. He'll leave them. He wants 'producer's money'; I guarantee you can get him. Will you do it, Michael, please?"

"In the future, Swanky, I would appreciate your requests a little more in advance."

"Oh, thank you, Michael. You're the best. If I see you at the Governor's Ball, and I'm drunk and you accidentally fondle my tits, I won't call the cops."

Idors laughs and ends the conversation. "Good luck tonight, Swanky."

Sandra, who has been listening to all this, folds up her tray and is ready to go. "Swanky?"

"Yes?"

"Did I just hear you being naughty?"

"Naughty? Just because I invited the guy to give my tits a little squeeze?"

"No. Naughty because you just double-crossed some person named Stanley."

Swanky gets up from the couch and goes to the bar. She takes a bottle of Evian from the refrigerator and opens it, then turns to Sandra. "C'mere."

Sandra crosses the room and sits on a barstool.

Swanky pours the Evian water into two very elegant champagne glasses, and hands one to Sandra. She then lifts her glass, salutes Sandra, and takes a sip. "I did not just double-cross some person named Stanley.

"What I just did was double-cross some person who spends some part of each and every day figuring out a way to double-cross me." Swanky takes another sip of water and smiles. "At the moment, the score is two-to-one . . . my favor.

"However, he still thinks the score is tied."

Sandra is still uncomfortable with Swanky's rationale. "But is that a good way to live?"

Swanky shrugs. "That depends on whether or not you want to be the one who moons the principal."

This remark causes Sandra to smile. "Okay, let's say you

do win the double-cross game . . . what is it you actually win?"

Swanky's expression hardens. "Fear and respect. Submission and compliance."

Swanky looks out at the Pacific Ocean churning waves onto her private beach. Then turns back to Sandra. "Those are the tactics and the prizes for winning this little war we call 'life.'"

Sandra smiles, picks up her folding table and manicure kit, and heads for the door where she stops, turns around, and speaks before leaving, "It seems like a lot of unpleasant stuff to go through . . . just to be famous."

"Sandra, where are you gonna be tonight when I leave my beautiful Malibu home and step into a sleek limousine which will chauffeur me to the Academy Awards where I will then be admired by billions of people . . . only hours before I am at an unbelievably glamorous party in Beverly Hills, laughing in the midst of the world's most famous celebrities . . . as I select my night's temporary stud muffin?"

Sandra answers, "I'll be sitting in front of my TV, thinking . . . *'If it were my Oscar speech, I'd just say thanks to my mom . . . and thanks to my dad.'*"

Sandra smiles at Swanky, opens the door, steps out, and closes the door behind her . . . but moments later re-opens the door, sticks her head back inside, and adds to her Oscar speech, "And thanks to my boyfriend, Charlton Preston, whose unwavering love and support made it possible for me to be here tonight."

Sandra takes a brief pause to enjoy her Oscar moment, then leaves. But then returns, steps back inside, and makes another little addition, "And my grandma and my grandpa, and my sisters Gina, Jenifer, and Pansy, and my brother Dale, and my cousins Nick, Nathan, Nicolo, Christopher, Emma, Stacie, and Kelly. And Aunt Susie. And my sister's husband Peter. And my sister-in-law Cindy. And Eric. And Whitney and Dave. And Mabel and Myrna. And Uncle Jake and Aunt Carolyn. And Uncle Terry . . . can't forget the guy who bought me my first pair of lime-green tennis shoes. And God. And my parents' best friends Ronnie, Johnny, and Bob. And especially my best friend Linda, and my second and third-best friends, Pammy and Sammy.

"So, good night, God bless you, and God bless America."

Sandra now waves and leaves, closing the door behind her.

Swanky takes a moment to let a few brief thoughts pass through her mind, then reaches over and takes a thumb-tacked cocktail napkin off the small message board behind the bar. She mumbles phone numbers off the napkin as she presses them into her speaker phone.

A man answers, "Hello."

"Hello. This is Swanky Shampane. Are you the man I met in the Chez Malibu Bar and Grill last week, Charlton Preston?"

"Swanky, you finally called."

"Yes. And though I'm quite sure you're already aware of it, I just wanted to tell you that you are a piece of slime and not worth the spit that I'll blow into your face if you ever again come within ten feet of me. "Have a rotten day."

Having said her piece, Swanky presses the phone off.

A few moments pass as Swanky calms herself. Then the phone rings again and Swanky answers, "Hello."

"Hello Swanky, this is Robert. I just started your taxes and right away, I can see we've got a problem. "You're going to need to sell some stock if you want to continue giving this kind of money to that abused-kids thing."

"Robert, you stupid shit! Why are you calling me on Oscar night with business?"

"I just wanted you to know, that's all."

"Think Robert. Oscar night. Once per lifetime. Not the best time to work on your taxes. Think, Robert! Think!"

Swanky immediately ends the conversation with an angry press of a button.

CHAPTER SEVENTEEN

The limousine, not looking quite as nice as it did when it was first delivered to Johnny, continues along Highway 395 through the Nevada desert. A back tail light is broken, the trunk is twisted out of shape, and a side mirror is blown apart and dangling from the door. And it's loud.

The inside is not so bad. The radio blares. Lucy Lee and Johnny, enjoying the ride, sing along with Elvis . . . "You ain't nothin' but a hound dog . . ."

The song concludes as a roadside vegetable stand comes into view. Having had his taste buds disrupted back at Wanda's cafe, Johnny is now extremely hungry and assumes Lucy Lee is too. "Wow. A vegetable stand. You must be hungry. You want some carrots or something? Celery?"

Lucy Lee is also extremely hungry. "Oh boy, yes."

The limousine pulls off the road. The vegetable stand

consists of ten baskets of vegetables shaded under a plastic tarp tied between two trees. A few vegetables from each basket are spread out on three fold-up tables.

They exit the limo. A Mexican man and his wife operate this stand while two children are at play near an old station wagon parked close by. The man greets his customers, "Good morning, amigo. Seniorita."

Johnny and Lucy Lee return his good-natured salutation, "Good morning."

"Just look around. Put what you want in a bag." The man indicates to a small stack of used brown paper bags on a fourth table, which is apparently used for business purposes.

Lucy Lee and Johnny smile and begin inspecting the vegetables. Johnny picks up a squash, looks it over, and gets Lucy Lee's attention as he gestures to its superb quality. "Look at this."

Lucy Lee, who has been inspecting the radishes at a different table, smiles, and nods in agreement.

Johnny now looks over to the Mexican man and pays him a fine compliment. "This is a very nice-looking squash."

The man smiles back, then, when Johnny's attention has returned to his inspection, he glances at his wife and rolls his eyes: "A good-looking squash?"

Lucy Lee has found a nice bunch of radishes and holds them up for Johnny to see. "Johnny, look."

Johnny is very impressed. "Wow."

Lucy Lee is anxious to deal. "How much are these?"

The man answers, "Three dollars a bag."

Lucy Lee is ready to bargain. "I'll give you two dollars a bag."

The man repeats himself, "Radishes are three dollars a bag."

She thinks it over. "I'll go two-fifty."

The man repeats himself again, "Three dollars."

"Two-seventy-five."

"Three dollars."

"Two-ninety."

"Three dollars."

"Two-ninety-five."

The man sighs. "Okay, you win. How many bags you want?"

"Nine."

The man goes to a basket and begins gathering together nine bags of radishes.

Lucy Lee moves over to the table where Johnny holds the squash. Johnny speaks to her in a confidential tone. "You really want nine bags of radishes?"

Lucy Lee steals a glance at the Mexican man before answering in a low voice, "At these prices, absolutely. In the city, you can't touch a bag of radishes of this caliber for less than four dollars."

Johnny nods and they head for the tomatoes and the cabbages.

* * *

An hour passes before they have loaded up their bargains and are back on the road. The radio blares, and their spirits are elevated as they sing "Respect" along with Aretha Franklin, and stuff themselves with fresh vegetables.

Because the opaque separation window is closed behind their heads, the passenger area cannot be seen.

Lucy Lee has appointed herself to be in charge of the food. "How about another radish?"

Johnny nods. "I love them, but I'm afraid of eating too many. They make me belch." Then he adds with a chuckle, "And I certainly wouldn't want to offend anybody on Oscar night."

Lucy Lee digs into one of the three brown paper bags at her feet and pulls out a bundle of scallions. "Onion?"

Johnny has the appetite of a horse. "Mmmmmmm. Yes please."

Lucy Lee takes the rubber bands off the bundle and hands the onions to Johnny. She then pulls another bundle from a bag, removes the rubber bands, and joins Johnny in the pleasure of eating fresh onions. They converse as they eat.

"My dad loved onions. He's the one who taught me how to bargain."

Johnny is impressed. "That was the first time I've ever tried it. Usually, I just pay whatever they tell me it costs."

"My dad said I was a natural at it."

Johnny changes the radio station and suddenly the Rolling Stones blast into the scene: "I can't get nooo sa-tis-fac-tion!"

Johnny and Lucy Lee waste no time snapping their fingers and joining in.

After a few verses, Johnny inquires as to the amount they saved by buying in bulk. "How much do you think we saved on the vegetables?"

Lucy Lee calculates. "Well, we saved approximately a dollar on every bag, so I'd say we probably saved about eighty bucks."

Johnny is pleasantly surprised. "That's a lot of money to save just on vegetables."

"My dad says, 'A penny saved is a penny earned, and a penny earned is a penny saved.'"

"Your dad sure knew a lot of things. What kind of work did he do?"

"He did many things. He was always trying to improve himself. At first, before my parents came to America, he worked in the rice fields.

"And then, once they got to America, he worked in a factory, and then he worked in a coal mine, and then a steel mill.

"And then, when he was seventy, he became a sky diving instructor . . . and then he inherited a lot of money and retired."

"Is he the one who taught you how to be a mechanic?"

"Yes. He said that no matter what you want to be, all you have to do is say it to yourself enough times, and one day you will become it.

"So, one night I kept saying to myself, *I want to be a mechanic,* over and over, for about eight hours, and then the next morning I was a mechanic."

"You didn't go to school for it or anything like that?"

"No. I just answered an ad in the newspaper for a mechanic who would work cheap. And then I got hired, and then I drove the boss to jail."

"You drove your boss to jail?"

"Yes. He had a bunch of parking tickets, and so he had to go to jail starting that very day he hired me."

"That's a pretty unique way of starting a job . . . driving your boss to jail."

"Not all the way. I just drove him part of the way, and then, from the intersection, the ambulance drove him the rest of the way.

"The police said he's lucky to be alive. But I'd say I'm pretty lucky too for getting a mechanic's job the first day I'd ever driven a car.

"Just like when I got a ski instructor's job the very first day I ever put on skis.

"So, I'd say I'm the lucky one. Just like my dad said."

A road sign reads: "LOS ANGELES 150 Miles."

CHAPTER EIGHTEEN

With hours still to pass before Swanky needs to shower and dress before her limousine arrives to whisk her off to the Oscars, she will relax by the pool. Carrying a bottle of drinking water, a Bloody Mary, and a beach bag, Swanky walks out of the house.

She sets the Bloody Mary down in the shade beneath Jimmy's chaise lounge as he speaks without opening his eyes, "I hope you're not gonna be splashing around while I'm trying to nap."

Swanky sits on an adjacent lounger and applies her sunscreen. "Have you ever seen me splash around?"

Jimmy mumbles, "Never."

"Then why would you think I might splash around today?"

"Nervousness."

"And why would I be nervous? I'm not gonna win, nobody likes me–what's to be nervous about?"

Swanky takes a sip of water and stretches out.

Jimmy opens one eye. "You got a speech ready?"

Swanky chuckles. "Don't worry, if I did win, I'd know exactly what to say."

"Would you thank me?"

"Yeah. Right after Ma and Pa."

"Why don't you take me as your date?"

"Because you're old, and you're chubby, and you've got hair growing out of your ears."

They both share a laugh at this brutal sort of humor. "Besides, I want you to watch it on television, so when I get home, you can give me your opinion of how I came across."

"Did you bring my mid-afternoon medicine?"

Swanky closes her eyes and tilts her chin upward to allow the sun's rays access to her neck. "It's under your lounger close to your butt."

"Am I gonna have to open both my eyes to find it?"

"Maybe, maybe not."

"Did you remember to put a straw in it?"

"No."

"The service is getting a little lax around here, have you noticed?"

"Try tipping a little better, see if things improve."

Without opening his eyes, Jimmy begins feeling around for his drink.

* * *

From inside Swanky's beach bag, an alarm clock goes off.

Swanky wakes from her nap, reaches inside the bag and shuts off the alarm, sits up, stretches, and looks over at Jimmy swimming leisurely about. She speaks, "Let's see, today is Monday, March the Ninth. What to do? What to do?"

She feigns a yawn and pats her mouth. "Maybe I'll go take a shower, have my hair done, have millions of dollars-worth of jewelry delivered to my front door, put on my new thirteen-thousand-dollar dress, get into a fabulous limousine, drive to the Dolby Theater, and mingle with the most famous movie stars in the world who are all gathered together to pay tribute to the nominees for best female actress . . . as media people from all over the globe clamor to take my picture and hear my voice . . . while billions and billions of fellow human beings from the planet Earth . . . watch. Enviously.

"Or maybe I'll just put on some old sweats, rent a movie, and have a pizza delivered."

Jimmy's face now takes on the beginnings of a smile that will rapidly work its way into uncontrollable laughter. "I'd prefer that you go mingle with the stars."

"Why is that?"

"Well, if you do, then maybe you could get me Victoria Blaine's autograph."

They both burst out laughing. And it goes on and on, until Swanky finally breaks it off, gets out of her lounger, picks up her beach bag, and speaks as she climbs the rock stairs back to the house. "It is quite likely that someday I will kill you with my bare hands."

Jimmy yells back at her. "Don't do it until I'm really old and decrepit!"

Swanky smiles and gives him a look: "Don't make me say it."

"Hey, I'm not decrepit yet! I've got at least three more erections left! I still haven't used up the one for 2007!"

* * *

Swanky takes a shower, listening to classical music, with a wide swath of ocean lapping peacefully onto the shore below the window in front of her naked body.

CHAPTER NINETEEN

Johnny and Lucy Lee continue along, singing with the radio and eating onions. Johnny looks at his wristwatch. "Well, it looks like we're just gonna make it on time. We're supposed to be at the Silver Stallion Limousine Service no later than four o'clock."

He puts another scallion into his mouth. "They're gonna give us our driving assignment and a map on how to get to the star's house . . . and then we just pick 'em up, drive 'em to the Oscars, wait for 'em, and then take 'em to a bunch of parties afterwards. This is gonna be fun."

Lucy Lee offers him another bundle of onions as she is finishing off her personal bundle.

Johnny hesitates. "Well, I probably ought to go easy on the onions, I don't want my breath to smell on Oscar night. Would you remind me to stop and get a pack of Lifesavers?"

"Wintergreen?"

"I was thinking of the other kind. The ones in the blue pack."

Lucy Lee would rather he get the kind she prefers. "Oh yeah, peppermint. They're really good too. They're second-best."

"Don't forget to remind me, okay?"

"I always remember things."

Johnny leans his face in close to her nose. "Would you smell my breath, please?"

Lucy Lee angles her nose even closer to his mouth. Johnny exhales a deep breath directly at her nose. "Can you smell the onions?"

"No. Your breath smells fine."

They both lean back to their vertical positions.

"Okay. Maybe I will have just one more bundle."

Lucy Lee digs into a brown paper bag. "How about a radish? They're better for you."

"Okay. Just a small one."

Lucy Lee pulls out a bundle of twenty to thirty radishes, takes off the rubber band, and hands it over.

He appreciates her help. "Thanks."

Lucy Lee turns the radio up a little and they join right in with the Beatles singing "Yesterday."

By now, it has been well-established that Johnny and Lucy Lee have two of the world's worst singing voices. However, even these two can't ruin this classic. Although, it is almost managed when, right after the part that goes, "Suddenly, I'm not half the man I used to be. There's a shadow hanging over me" . . . Johnny releases a very long and loud belch. "Excuse me. I didn't do that on purpose. I never could control my radishes. It just seems to happen on its own. I sure hope it doesn't happen tonight."

CHAPTER TWENTY

Swanky sits in her bathrobe, in her boudoir, in front of a large vanity mirror lit up by many bulbs. She attends to the first stage of her makeup.

The buzz from the front-gate intercom is heard. Swanky answers on a nearby intercom, "Hello."

A man's voice follows, "Hi. It's me."

Swanky presses a button to buzz him in, and momentarily, a hip young hairdresser enters her boudoir, carrying what appears to be an elaborate hat box.

Swanky shows some concern. "Mauricio, are you still fresh?"

"Yes, I am still fresh."

"How many heads have you done today?"

"Eight."

"Eight heads and you're still fresh?"

Mauricio assures her, "Yes. I am still fresh. I am young."

Swanky has other concerns. "Who did you do?"

Mauricio rolls the tension out of his neck and shoulders. "I did Winslet, Aniston, Reese . . . Skyes, Viola, McDormand . . . Bullock . . . and . . . I did someone else. I can't remember who. I have been doing six or seven heads a day for the last two weeks. Parties, pre-Oscar shows, nominee interviews . . . it has been crazy, crazy, crazy."

Swanky gets to the point. "The eighth head must have been Victoria Blaine's. Entertainment Tonight said that you were the one who was going to be doing her hair."

"Oh my gosh, can you imagine I forgot that I did Victoria Blaine's hair? Lord Almighty, there is one to write home about . . . 'Dear Mother, I have been so busy that I forgot to tell you that on the night of the Academy Awards I did the hair of the greatest actress in the world.'"

Swanky gives Mauricio a piercing look. He immediately realizes his blunder and attempts to rectify it, "Along with the other greatest actress . . . Swanky Shampane." Swanky stares him down before he changes the subject, "How would you like your hair tonight? Up and back? Down and forward? Down and back? Off to the side?"

Swanky interrupts him, "I want you to do it exactly like Blaine's . . . only better."

Mauricio protests. "Oh Swanky no, no, no. I could never do that. It would not be ethical."

"Mauricio, how much are you getting for doing my hair?

"You know how much. Everything is double during Oscar week. Everyone charges the same. Double."

Swanky nods. "Eight hundred. Plus tip. Pretty good money for an hour's work."

She considers the 'arrangement.' "I'd be willing to pay three thousand. Plus tip. If I could only find somebody to do it the way I want it."

Mauricio considers the 'opportunity.' "I can do it, sort of, but I have to make it a little different."

"No. I want it exactly the same. Only better."

Mauricio is caught between a moral rock and an ethical hard place. "But people will know. They will see you both together, and they will know."

"No, they won't. We're seated ten rows apart. Nobody will even notice."

"Yes, they will!"

"No!!! They won't!!!"

Mauricio sighs.

CHAPTER TWENTY-ONE

The limousine loudly passes a highway sign: "LOS ANGELES 50 MILES."

Lucy Lee and Johnny still munch on onions and radishes, and still sing enthusiastically along with the radio: "Oh Suzannah, don't you cry for me . . . 'cause I come from Alabama, with a banjo on my knee . . ."

Johnny turns the radio down. "You really have a nice voice. You could be a singer. Professionally, I mean."

Lucy Lee is humbled. Momentarily. "Thank you. I've been thinking about it. I'd like to be a singer, and a dancer, in the movies."

Johnny is a voice of encouragement. "Like Ginger Rogers?"

"Shirley Temple."

Johnny adjusts his encouragement. "Oh, are you a tap dancer too?"

"Well, not professionally or anything like that, but my dad says my toes have natural rhythm. It runs in our family."

Johnny tries to support her dream. "Wouldn't it be great if you were the star of a tap dance movie, and then won an Oscar? You could tap dance out onto the stage to make your Oscar speech."

Lucy maintains her humility. "Gosh, if I ever won an Oscar, I'd be too darn nervous to even make a speech. I'd probably just thank my dad for teaching me the value of self-confidence."

She smiles sweetly and adds, "I'd rather be the one watching on television, the one the star thanks by name. Because then you'd always know that you really meant a lot to them."

Johnny agrees, "Yeah, that would be a wonderful way to honor somebody. I'd probably just thank my mom and dad, and thank the best school teacher I ever had."

"What was his name?"

"I forget."

"Did you have a nice childhood?"

Lucy proceeds to fall in love with Johnny as he tells her about his family, "I had a great childhood. I grew up on a little farm out in the middle of the Nevada desert.

"The pace was kind of slow but there was a lot to do. We had a reservoir to swim in, and I had my own dog, and there was a gigantic cottonwood tree where my dad and I built a treehouse when I was five years old.

"And on bread day, my mom would put a huge slice of warm

bread with ice-cold pats of butter on it . . . inside a brown paper bag with my name on it.

"And then she'd take a clothespin and clip the bag to the clothesline which ran from our back porch all the way up to my treehouse . . . and then she'd ring a bell . . . and I'd hear it . . . and I'd start reeling up the clothesline.

"And when you're that young, it seems like the bread is never gonna arrive . . . but then later, when I was in my teens, I could get that bread from the back porch into my hands in about twenty seconds.

"And my mom would count the seconds out loud for me. One time, I did it in fourteen seconds. That was my best time ever. Last year, when I went home for Thanksgiving, it took me about two minutes.

"But that was just because I was teasing my mom."

Lucy Lee is fascinated by this story. "Did she laugh?"

Johnny chuckles. "Well . . . it was cold, and she wanted to get back inside to her kitchen and finish making her pumpkin pie . . . but I just pulled the clothesline real slowly, and she just kept counting."

Lucy Lee is curious, "Why didn't she just go back inside."

"She couldn't. Because one time, in the hospital, on the day I fell out of the tree and broke my legs, she took my hand and looked me in the eyes, and said, 'Anytime you're back in that tree and pulling my bread up to you . . . I'll be there on the back porch counting for you.'"

Lucy Lee appreciates her commitment to keeping her word. "So, she was kind of trapped. She had to stay. She'd given her word."

"Yeah. So, I just pulled real slow. Ninety-three seconds . . . ninety-four . . . ninety-five . . . ninety-six . . ."

Johnny grins. "My mom was a pretty serious person. She never had much time for joking around . . . but that day, even though she looked like she was getting annoyed . . . I could tell she was laughing on the inside."

Lucy Lee is hooked. "I'd like to meet your parents."

Johnny smiles. "I wish you could. But I lost them fifty-three days ago. First my mom, then three hours later, my dad."

"Were you there when they died?"

"Yes."

"Good."

CHAPTER TWENTY-TWO

Swanky sits on a bar stool watching a pre-Oscar television show. Her hair looks great.

On the screen, two popular entertainment hosts stand in a media area with microphones in their hands.

One speaks, "Well, as you would imagine, the excitement is growing by the minute. In just about one hour, the first stars will be arriving.

"They will step out of their limousines down there at the end of the red carpet, and will take that time-honored walk up to the theater with thousands of screaming fans in the bleachers on one side, some having camped out for over two weeks just to get seats, and thousands of media people on the other side just trying to get pictures or a quick interview, or especially, that controversial little sound bite that someone lucky enough to be in the right place at the right time is surely going to get."

The other host chimes in, "Who are you hoping to see tonight?"

"To be perfectly honest with you, if I see Victoria Blaine, I will consider this to be one of the most, if not thee most, exciting night of my life."

Swanky picks up the remote control and clicks the television off.

Jimmy enters, looks at Swanky, gives her 'two thumbs up,' "Wow!!!" then goes directly to the bar and fixes himself a drink. He has changed out of his swimsuit and into leisure clothes. He is fresh from a shower and looks quite healthy and dapper for a man in his eighties. He speaks to Swanky, "There's a bunch of pre-Oscar shows on now."

Swanky responds, "No there aren't."

Jimmy makes an observation, "Let me guess. There actually are many pre-Oscar shows on now, but they all seem to mention the 'B' word more than you care to hear it . . . so, in this house, there are no pre-Oscar shows on now. Correct?"

Swanky grunts. "What's with that filthy bitch. She's got all these media people eating out of her hand."

Jimmy stirs his drink and takes a sip. "How about letting the Jimster make you a nice little Martini? It'd be good for your nerves."

"I don't think so, Jimster. Except for losing the Oscar, I expect to have an absolutely perfect night. I've worked my ass off for it, and I'm certainly not going to let a little booze screw it up."

"That's why you're not taking me to the Oscars, isn't it? You think I'd get drunk and embarrass you."

Swanky smiles. "At what time do you intend to be drunk tonight?"

"The usual."

"Six-thirty?"

"Maybe six-forty-five. I got kind of a late start today."

Swanky stands and kisses him on top of the head. She then walks into the kitchen, opens the refrigerator, takes out a bundle of celery, breaks off a single stalk, rinses it, breaks that stalk in half, returns the bundle to the refrigerator, and rejoins Jimmy at the bar where she slowly consumes her half-stalk of celery.

She then moves onto the couch without wrinkling her dress. "Tonight, everything is going to be perfect. Almost."

Jimmy tries to be supportive. "Hey, you might win."

Swanky grumbles. "Yeah, and your aunt might be your uncle if only she had a pair of nuts."

Jimmy stares at the weathered sign behind the bar: "When all life seems to be offering you is one big fat lemon . . . grab the sonofabitch . . . and make yourself some fuckin' lemonade." "Swanky, don't you think it's time you took down this old sign and put up a Picasso or something?"

Swanky defines her personal feelings about the sign, "I acquired that sign the day I changed my name and started a new life. The day I die will be the first chance anybody will ever have to remove that sign from that wall."

Swanky takes a bottle of mineral water from behind the bar, opens it, and continues the history of the sign, "On my nineteenth birthday, the girls I worked with gave me that sign."

"What exactly does that sign mean to you?"

"It means that in this life there's a lot of lousy stuff that's gonna be inflicted upon you. But if you refuse to accept it, if you just keep your head up whenever you feel like crying . . . then you can beat the pain. You can survive. It's just another layer of scar tissue.

"That's exactly what that sign says to me. It reminds me of the way to deal with the pain.

"But if the pain is ripping you apart from the inside . . . you might just have to spit, hard, into the face of your own self-hatred.

"And that's the pain I'm afraid of. So far I've been lucky . . . I've always been able to make the lemonade."

Jimmy is sympathetic. "And that's how you deal with life's cruel little jokes?"

Swanky stands up and gently touches the sign. "That's what took me from a cathouse in Nevada to a beach house in Malibu."

The intercom buzzes and Swanky answers, "Hello."

A man's voice replies, "Harry Winston delivery."

Swanky buzzes him in.

As she quick-steps across the room to open the front door, she smiles back over her shoulder to Jimmy and shakes her fanny. "Excuse me while I let in my jewelry guy . . . he's got a few million bucks worth of that sparkly stuff for me."

Jimmy likes to see her in a relaxed mood. Swanky opens the door and invites a fashionably dressed large man and his two armed guards inside, one of whom is carrying a vase of twelve long-stemmed red roses. "Entrée, gentlemen."

They enter, and the large man takes a short contract from his coat pocket and offers it for Swanky to sign, along with the gold pen he extends to her.

Swanky gives it a quick perusal, then signs it. The man takes a sterling silver jewelry case out of another coat pocket, hands it to Swanky, and speaks as he places the vase of roses on the coffee table, "Mr. Winston wishes you the very best of luck tonight."

"Please tell Mr. Winston that I love his hands, and his feet and his head, and mostly, I love his style."

The men depart. Swanky closes the door and smiles at Jimmy. "Is there no end to how perfect this night is going to be?"

CHAPTER TWENTY-THREE

A limousine cruises along the Santa Monica freeway, turns off on Pico Blvd, travels a short distance, and pulls into a fenced parking lot at the Silver Stallion Limousine Service.

Johnny speaks to Lucy Lee before getting out and hurrying off toward the office, "Would you get my tuxedo out of the trunk while I'm in there? Thanks."

Johnny walks briskly toward the door with the sign "DISPATCHER" hanging above it. He enters and approaches a long counter where six employees are at work.

Bobby Rico, Brooklyn-born and aggressive, sporting a full head of remarkably stylish silver hair, seems to be running the operation, even though he is presently sneezing and will continue to sneeze throughout this entire scene. Johnny approaches him, "Excuse me. I'm supposed to talk to a guy named Bobby Rico."

"I'm Rico. You the guy Ralph sent down from Reno?"

"Yes."

"You're late. You're lucky I'm short of vehicles or I wouldn't even use you. How the hell can you be late on Oscar night?"

"Sorry."

"You brought a tux didn't you?"

"Yes. It's out in the limo."

Rico turns to the wall-size map of Beverly Hills strategically positioned at the end of the counter where all employees can approach it when searching for streets and planning routes. He talks to the man on his left without taking his eyes off the map, "Who's next on 'standby'?"

"Cerzyk Stoyanovich. Director, Best Foreign Film. Beverly Hills Hotel, Bungalow seven."

Together, they approach the map.

Rico chooses a route. "I think it's about time we circle behind and come in over Beverly Glen." He then yells over to one of his staff, "Al! How does the 405 look between Santa Monica and the valley?"

Al checks the screen on his computer. "Not too bad right at the moment. In half an hour, it'll be a crawl. But that's still a lot better than fighting the stop-and-go on Wilshire. If he leaves right now, he can probably just make it."

Rico yells, "Print it." He then turns back to give Johnny his instructions as Al fiddles with the map computer to trace out the chosen route. "Okay, we got ya a nice little run. Easy to find. Just don't get lost on one of them little side streets. But if you do, then call us immediately, and we'll tell you how to get out of there. Our number is on the map you're gonna get here in a second."

Suddenly, one of the guys at the far end of the counter drops his phone, jumps up from his desk, and yells out to Rico, "Bobby! Paul Gregory's on the phone! He's broken down on the Coast Highway! He says there's no way he can get to Swanky Shampane's!"

Rico goes ballistic. He charges down to the guy's desk, snatches up the phone, and screams into it, "How the fuck can a hundred and fifty fuckin' thousand dollar fuckin' vehicle break the fuck down!"

Rico now beats the phone violently five or six times against the desk. Then yells over to Al, "Reprint the Shampane map!"

Al hits a few buttons and a map glides through the printer. He immediately hands it over to Rico. Rico runs it up to Johnny. "Here! You're goin' to Malibu!"

Johnny takes the map with Rico still screaming at him, "Go! Go! You're already late!"

Johnny hurries out the door.

Rico is in despair, and slumps down into his director's chair, muttering to his staff, "I hate the Oscars. I hate the Oscars. Except for the money, I hate the Oscars."

Al turns to address the other staff members, "Did that guy stink, or what?!"

Everybody answers emphatically, "Yeah."

Al speaks to Rico, who appears to be shocked to find out about Johnny's odor.

Al comments, "I'm really surprised that you sent him out smelling like that."

Rico rages, "How the hell was I supposed to know! I can't smell nuttin'! My nose is plugged up! Why didn't you say sumpin'?! You fuckin' fuck-headed fuckers!"

* * *

Carrying a tuxedo, Johnny races around the corner of a gas station and darts into the men's room.

The limousine soon whizzes down the freeway. But, upon close observation, it doesn't look so good: busted tail light, twisted trunk, and trashed side-mirror.

Johnny speaks to Lucy Lee, "I think you gave me the wrong tuxedo."

Lucy Lee looks him over. "Yes. I gave you the small, I should have given you the large. You want to stop and change?"

Johnny checks his wristwatch. "No time, we're already late."

Lucy Lee accepts their predicament. "Thank heaven I didn't give you the extra small. That would have looked even more stupid."

Johnny is in total agreement. "Yeah."

Lucy Lee has something on her mind. "Johnny, do you remember this morning when you said you were afraid of me?"

"Yes."

"What did you mean?"

"I just meant that I was afraid that you might be a lot luckier than me, even though I don't believe in luck."

"And?"

"And that is . . . of some concern to me."

"You think I might hurt you?"

"Not on purpose . . . but I think we should be sort of . . . more careful when we're together around sharp objects. Or guns. Or dynamite. Or, you know, stuff like that. Cars. Power tools. Rat poison."

"I know what you're saying . . . 'lucky people are never very careful . . . so when you're around a lucky person you've got to have luck that is just as good as theirs, because if it isn't . . . you could get hurt.' So, from now on, I'm going to be extra careful."

"Thanks."

* * *

The limo races along the Pacific Coast Highway, headed for Malibu. Broken bits of glass and plastic fly off the limo as the roar of not having a muffler while going eighty MPH brings additional unwanted attention to their predicament, but not everything is disheartening.

Lucy Lee has found a silver cloud in the lining. "I am so excited."

"Why?"

"Oscar night. An ocean drive. Music to sing along with. I don't know. Just being alive I guess."

CHAPTER TWENTY-FOUR

Jimmy sips a Martini. Swanky paces the floor with growing frustration. "Where the hell's my limousine?!"

Jimmy stays calm. "Try to relax. I'm sure it'll be here any second."

Jimmy reaches for the telephone as he reads a number off a business card thumbtacked to the message board. "I'll call just to make sure. Stay calm. Have a drink."

Jimmy makes a call and a man's voice answers, "Silver Stallion Limousine Service."

"Hello, I'm calling for Swanky Shampane. It's after five o'clock. Her limousine was supposed to be here at four-thirty. Do we have a problem?"

"I'm terribly sorry. There was a vehicle malfunction, but we've already dispatched another vehicle, and it should be arriving any minute. We are so sorry and there will be no charge for tonight's service."

Jimmy says, "Thank you," hangs up, and turns to Swanky. "Minor delay. No problem. Stay calm, let me fix you a little drink."

"No! You know what alcohol does to me."

"It'll calm you down."

"No! It turns me into a raving asshole. No booze for me on Oscar night. Tonight, I'm gonna show the world that I am a much nicer person than they have been led to believe."

Swanky crosses her arms. "Tonight, the media is going to see a Swanky Shampane who is sweet, sincere, and thoroughly adorable. Just like the girl next door.

"Tonight, I intend to charm the living shit out of the fuckers."

* * *

At the massive CCA complex, Stanley stands in front of the floor-to-ceiling windows overlooking *the Avenue of the Stars*. He is troubled.

Before long, a smartly dressed man walks into the office without knocking. "We just got nailed. Cecil Clay. Our guy! Our nominee! Ditches us to sign with Idors! On Oscar night! We look bad on this one, Stan. Real bad."

Stanley sighs heavily. "Meeting tomorrow morning, nine o'clock, all the guys. It's time to start putting our knees into his balls."

CHAPTER TWENTY-FOUR

* * *

Jimmy freshens his martini. The intercom buzzes. Jimmy answers, "Hello."

A man's voice responds, "Flowers for Swanky Shampane."

Jimmy buzzes the front gate open, crosses the living room to a marble stand next to the front door, opens a decorative box, extracts a fifty dollar bill from the assorted denominations available, opens the front door, hands the fifty dollar tip to the delivery boy, and brings in a large arrangement of flowers.

He places the flowers on the coffee table, sits, and reads the sender's card: 'To the girl next door. Good luck tonight. Love Laura.'

Swanky smiles. The intercom buzzes again. Again Jimmy answers, "Hello."

Johnny responds, "Good evening. Your limousine is here."

"Ms. Shampane will be right out."

Jimmy gives Swanky a thumbs up.

Swanky picks up her beaded-pearl cosmetic purse, takes one last look in the mirror, turns to Jimmy, lifts her chin, stretches out her neck, and slowly revolves her face into an elegant profile. "Are my nipples level?"

Jimmy smiles. "Perfectly. Tonight, the world is yours. Good luck, darling."

Swanky blows him a kiss as she leaves the room. "Don't forget to pray for Victoria to trip on her way to the podium."

Jimmy chuckles, closes the door, takes a seat at the bar, and turns on a pre-Oscar show.

The television screen comes into focus showing stars already arriving at the Dolby Theater, walking down the red carpet, waving to fans, and offering a few words to the multitude of microphones being competitively thrust at them.

Suddenly, a frightening scream comes from outside Swanky's front door, and she immediately reappears, looking dazed and confused.

She motions for Jimmy to 'take a look' out there, as she heads for the bar where she immediately swigs down a hefty gulp of Jack Daniels.

Jimmy goes outside, returns a few seconds later, also appearing to be in a state of dazed confusion.

Swanky demands answers, "Did you see him?!"

Jimmy nods. "Yes."

"Did you smell him?!"

Jimmy nods again. "Yes."

"Why does my limousine look like a piece of shit . . . with a big banana on it?!"

"I don't know."

Swanky screams, "It's Stanley! Stanley did this to me!"

Jimmy needs to calm her down. "No, no! It's not Stanley's doing! It just happened this way! That's all! Nobody could have done this on purpose! It just happened!"

He instantly searches desperately through his pockets.

"Try to stay calm! There's nothing to do about it now! It's too late! You've got to get to the Oscars! It's only a ride; it's only transportation!"

He finally locates a pill container, opens it, and fumbles out a pill. "Here, take this. It'll calm you down."

Swanky snatches the container out of his hand and gulps down a handful of pills, and with the bottle of Jack Daniels in hand, stomps off to her waiting limousine, snarling as she goes, "Some dirty, rotten, stinkin, lousy, son of a bitchin bastard is gonna pay for this! So help me God!"

From inside the house, with the front door still yanked open, the limousine can be heard starting up and pulling away . . . very, very loudly.

Jimmy collapses slowly back onto the couch.

CHAPTER TWENTY-FIVE

The limo turns onto the Coast Highway and heads to the Oscars.

Before long, Lucy Lee thinks a little music might ease the tension. "Hey, what's that really cool song called, from that neat Victoria Blaine movie?

Johnny shrugs. "I dunno."

"Oh yeah, now I remember." And of course, she is inclined to sing it, with gusto. "Mama . . . Mama Mia, Mama Mia–"

The separation window slides down and Swanky's fuming face emerges, roaring at Lucy Lee, "Shaddup!!!"

She then snarls directly into Johnny's splinted ear, "And you!!! What's with the fuckin' veggies?!!!"

Now, for the first time, the passenger area reveals eighty brown paper bags, all brimming with vegetables, surrounding the only available sitting place.

Johnny twists his neck to look back at Swanky and explain things . . . but regrettably, when he opens his mouth to speak, words do not come out.

Instead of an actual verbal explanation, Swanky is subjected to one very long and sonorous belch.

Johnny is fraught with remorse. "Sorry."

Swanky just looks at him, then speaks in trembling tones, "Drive me as close to the Dolby Theater as you can get, let me out in an alley where nobody can see me, then get the hell away from me."

Swanky takes a long swig from her bottle of Daniels as the separation window slides back up.

* * *

The limo, dangling, twisted, and battered, with Potato Butt Johnson's large yellow plumbing sign strapped to its roof, rolls thunderously into Santa Monica and merges with the dense traffic.

Johnny has a concern and speaks in a low voice to Lucy Lee, "When we get there, am I supposed to get out and open the door for her?"

Lucy Lee, a stickler for time-honored protocols, advises him, "I think that would be a very nice gesture."

Johnny suddenly remembers something. "I forgot to get Lifesavers."

Lucy Lee shares the blame. "Both of us did."

Johnny suddenly remembers something else. "We also forgot to wash the car."

Lucy Lee shares Johnny's mistake. "You can do it tomorrow when we get home. I'll help you."

* * *

They are now in the dreaded crawl-speed traffic when the separation window glides down and Swanky growls instructions, "Go left at the corner, and let me out in the first alleyway you come to!"

Then the separation window immediately glides back to its closed position.

Johnny makes a left turn at the corner, travels halfway down the street, turns into an alleyway, and stops.

The window glides back down and again Swanky issues instructions, "Get out and see if anybody's around."

Johnny gets out and looks around. Then gets back in. "The coast is clear."

Swanky tells them exactly what to do next, "All right. I'm gonna get out. As soon as I do, you drive away. And do not, I repeat, do not tell a single person, ever, that you drove me to the Academy Awards. Or I will hunt you down, cut off your balls, and feed them to a buzzard! Do you understand?"

"Yes ma'am."

CHAPTER TWENTY-FIVE

The separation window slides shut.

Lucy Lee's animated hands now get Johnny's attention, 'shooing' him out of the limo. He understands: he should open the door for Ms. Shampane.

Johnny gets out and opens her door.

But just as Swanky steps out, two officers in a police car turn into the alleyway.

Swanky spots them and jumps back into the limo, yanking Johnny in with her and slamming the door shut behind them.

Diving onto the floor, Swanky screams at Johnny, "Lock the doors! Hide me!"

Johnny slams down the door locks and begins frantically pouring bags of vegetables over Swanky.

The police car drives slowly up to the limo. The officers get out and cautiously approach the vehicle.

An officer speaks to the only person available, "Having car trouble?"

Lucy Lee answers politely, "No."

"You're going to have to move your vehicle. This is a restricted, parking-only alley."

Lucy Lee appreciates the rigors inherent to being an officer of the law and is glad to follow their wishes. "Yes sir."

She slides over into the driver's seat as the officers get back into their car. Lucy Lee puts the limo in gear and steps on the gas. But once again, she has mistakenly put it into reverse.

Lurching backwards, the limo smashes into the concrete

wall behind her. Sounds like, "Thud! And fuuuck!" come from the limo's two backseat passengers.

Lucy Lee, anxious to rectify matters, promptly shifts gears, steps on the gas, and the limo instantly vaults back across the alley into a different concrete wall, provoking more of the same sounds, but louder.

She quickly shifts back into reverse, propelling the limo back against the first concrete wall and causing a slight change in language: "Dang! Shit-fuck!"

Then, it's immediately back into the second wall for the second time. (The vehicle is now noticeably shorter than it was a few seconds ago.)

The two police officers jump out of their patrol car and run up to the limo. One grabs the driver's door and yanks it open. "What's the matter with you?!!! Don't you know how to drive!?"

Through the forming tears, Lucy Lee's sweetness and innocence prevail. "I do, but I'm just nervous because my friend is supposed to drive Ms. Shampane to the Academy Awards, but we got stuck in traffic, and then we came down this alley, and then–"

The officer interrupts her, "You've got Swanky Shampane in the back of this limo?"

"Yes. And we're late getting her to the Oscars and–"

The officer takes a quick look at his wristwatch and shouts over to his partner, "Frank! Run interference for me! The Dolby Theater! Emergency!"

Pushing Lucy Lee headfirst across the seat, the officer jumps into the limo and tears off close behind the speeding police car. Lights are flashing and sirens are blaring.

After screeching around four or five corners, and maneuvering through several roped-off areas, the loud and battered limousine comes to a sudden stop at the end of the red carpet where the fans and media are jolted into a heightened frenzy of anticipation.

And after a brief period, this limousine, with the bright yellow sign on its roof touting Potato Butt Johnson's ability to get your bowels flowing again, fails to immediately unload any passengers.

Eventually, the police officer gets out of the vehicle and dramatically opens a back door . . . at which point Swanky tumbles out onto the red carpet.

She looks as though she has just been dislodged from a clothes dryer. Her hair points in all directions, one earring is missing, and so is one shoe. Her dress is torn and crumpled and streaked with tomato stains. She is also drunk, drugged, and reeking of onions. She also has a clump of barf stuck in her hair.

However, the show must go on. And, as Johnny steps out of the limousine behind her, knocking a couple of cabbages onto the ground in the process, Swanky struggles to her feet, takes his arm, and begins the long walk down the red carpet between the delirious fans and the astonished media . . . dignified and proud.

It is a walk that is somewhat precarious due to the single high-heel shoe that pitches her sideways at every step.

The hushed crowd appears to be extremely eager to hear 'the spin' that Swanky is about to put on 'her entrance.'

Directing her voice towards an army of reporters holding microphones, Swanky smiles and turns lemons into lemonade. "I hope you all enjoyed this little bit of 'live theater' that I created . . . just for you."

She then notices a scallion lodged in the depths of her cleavage, pulls it out, and flings it to her fans. "This is my personal statement on the preposterous notion of . . . 'celebrity.'"

Under the loud response of the adoring crowd, reporters ask questions, "What does that mean?" "Who's your new boyfriend?" "How long have you two been seeing each other?"

Having made her statement, Swanky now heads off toward the front entrance of the Dolby Theater on the arm of her stupidly dressed, limping chauffeur with the splinted ear and fingers.

Mary Hart addresses a camera, "Well, there you have it. Swanky Shampane has probably just made the Academy Awards' most memorable entrance ever . . . proving in no uncertain terms that she emphatically deserves her reputation as one of Hollywood's gutsiest and most charming stars."

Mary then lifts an eyebrow and smiles. "Not exactly your girl next door . . . but nevertheless . . . a fabulous star."

CHAPTER TWENTY-SIX

Back in Reno, as Monty stands at a large kitchen table covered with food, watching members of his wife's family load up their plates, the Oscar show is heard from the television in the living room. A winner is about to be announced.

"And the winner for Best Cinematographer is . . . Cecil Clay . . . for *The Road to Jack's House*."

Applause follows as Cecil walks to the podium to make his Oscar speech.

Things quiet down as Cecil begins, "I can't believe this is really happening. I don't know what to say. I didn't think I was going to win so I don't really have anything prepared.

"Let me just thank the members of the Academy from the bottom of my heart for their recognition of my work. Now, maybe somebody will trust me enough to shoot a film with Victoria Blaine or Swanky Shampane.

"Thank you all very much. Thank you."

Monty is resigned to the large quantities of food being consumed in his kitchen, yet feels compelled to speak as his brother-in-law piles a particularly high mound of food onto his plate, "Hey Larry, wait a second, you can still fit another pea on there."

From the living room, a woman's voice calls out. "Hey, in the kitchen, hurry up. They're almost ready to announce Best Actress."

Everybody moves into the living room and gets seated as Billy Crystal's voice introduces the final nominee in the Best Actress category. As Crystal speaks, Monty pulls a dog-eared sheet of paper from his pocket and reads from it. "Eddie, I got you for a mallard on Blaine at eight to five. Hank, you're down for twenty on McDormand at six to one. Ron, you got half a yard on Sykes at eight to one. And Larry, you and Wall Street Bob got Shampane at forty to one ... for two bucks apiece."

Crystal continues, "And now, the final nominee in the Best Actress category, Victoria Blaine, for her role in *The Mississippi Spy*."

The customary clip from the nominee's film plays:

In a dark and dank jail cell, with a single light bulb hanging over Victoria Blaine's head, a Nazi officer menaces her with a heavy German accent, " So, Miss Mary Johnson from Tupelo Mississippi ... this rope around your neck is going to get tighter . . . much tighter . . . unless you give us zee name of zee American spy who stole our secrets. So, I ask you again . . . what is zee filthy traitor's name?!"

With her plantation petticoat ripped across the bodice to tastefully expose a glimpse of her throbbing breasts, Victoria speaks in a most charming Southern accent, "I will never, ever . . . betray my country. You may hang me at your earliest convenience . . . sir."

The clip ends and Crystal reappears. He is ready to keep the evening rolling but must first submit to the audience's protracted applause in tribute to Victoria's brilliant performance.

Crystal speaks, "To present the Oscar for best actress is last year's winner, Annette Bening."

Annette walks across the stage, takes the envelope, smiles, and opens it. "And the winner is . . . Swanky Shampane for *Inglorious Bitches.*

* * *

In Monty's living room, everybody appears to be in shock, especially Monty. Yanking his wallet out of his pocket, Monty storms back into the kitchen to pay off Larry at forty-to-one as Larry is currently busy loading up another heaping plate of chicken legs.

In the living room, everyone is frozen in their seat, with their eyes glued to the television set.

Every camera at the Dolby Theater is trained on the seat in the front row next to Victoria Blaine . . . where Swanky Shampane is passed out with her limbs askew and her head back, snoring with her mouth open . . . 'honking like a duck.'"

At the podium, Annette continues as if everything is progressing along very nicely, "And here to accept the award for Ms. Shampane is the new man in her life . . . Mr. Johnny Johnson."

Monty, hearing the name Johnny Johnson, staggers back into the living room, and his jaw drops open like everyone else's as Johnny steps out from the wings, pulls out the script from inside his tuxedo jacket, crosses the stage to the podium, and accepts Swanky's Oscar for her. Then, as the camera closes in on his face, he makes an Oscar speech, "I'd just like to thank my mother and father, without whose love and understanding I would not be here today. And I would also like to thank my best friend, Lucy Lee. And God Bless America, and everyone else in the entire world."

The applause is thunderous as Johnny lays his script on the podium and adds one final comment, "I'll just leave my script here for Steven Spielberg. It is about how to save the world."

Johnny now holds the Oscar over his head and walks triumphantly off the stage.

Outside the theater, Lucy Lee sits in the back of the limousine amidst the vegetables, watching the Oscar telecast on a small television screen. And, having just experienced Johnny honoring her by name, is now crying buckets of happy tears.

Across town at Myrna's Oscar party, everyone in attendance stares silently at the television screen with their mouths still open in response to Johnny showing his face at Myrna's party.

After an extended time, one of the party-goers addresses herself to the woman seated next to a tall, dark, and handsome aerobics instructor. "Rita . . . what just happened?"

Rita's face is a mask of frozen disbelief. "I . . . need . . . a drink."

CHAPTER TWENTY-SEVEN

The stars are loading into limos and heading off for the parties.

One limousine idles with a chauffeur standing alongside an open door. Stanley leans against the limo and makes a call on his cell phone. It is answered by a secretary's pre-recorded message, "Hello, you have reached the offices of Idors International Management. We are closed for the day. You may leave a message now."

Stanley speaks, "This message is for Michael Idors from Stanley Howard.

"Quite a night wasn't it? Sorry I missed you at the Governor's Ball. It was a great one. And now I'm headed off to Elton's, and after that to Clooney's breakfast party. And, as usual, I expect both will have excellent food and provide lots of laughs. Especially this time around.

"And by the way asshole, we want Cecil Clay back, before noon tomorrow, by way of a public statement given to the press, by Clay, from the front entrance at CCA. And that statement must say that he is . . .

". . . and here I want you to make certain that he uses this exact phrase . . . he is . . . '*very grateful to CCA for allowing him to return.*'

"And Mikey, if you should choose to be uncooperative on this matter . . . then I would strongly urge you to watch the next edition of The Hollywood Insider . . . because they might just play, and re-play, a phone call, which seems to suggest that the so-called 'special relationship' that exists between Michael Idors and his loyal clientele . . . leaves just a teeny bit to be desired . . . specifically the relationship with your sweet, wholesome, little country girl from the Wisconsin dairy farm.

"At least that's my opinion. Why don't you listen to the tape and then decide for yourself whether or not you want to send Clay off to humbly, and publicly, thank CCA for allowing the little prick to return?"

A beep sounds and the message about to be heard has been culled from a 'familiar' phone conversation recorded earlier in the day. Swanky's voice is heard, "Hello."

Then Stanley's voice is heard, "It's me, Swanky. I just want to go over this thing one more time. You saying that you would have no problem leaving that jerkoff Idors and coming back to CCA, is that correct?"

Swanky is heard repeating what she had said to Stanley earlier in the day, "That's right, Stanley, assuming of course that you quit giving those brainless, skinny-ass, no-talent, plastic-titted, smiley-faced mannequins the first look at any girl-next-door role that's worth half a shit."

The tape now clicks off.

And Stanley makes one final comment, "And Mikey, if you wouldn't mind, give Swanky a message for me. Tell her not to be too upset if that tape gets played now and then, here and there, around carefully selected Hollywood people.

"And also tell her that, as I see things, the score is two to two, and once again, all tied up. Sweet dreams."

CHAPTER TWENTY-EIGHT

Jimmy sits on a deck chair watching the ocean lunge softly at the beach below him. It is a starry night and the full moon throbs in all its splendor.

Before long, Jimmy looks up at the moon and raises his hands as if to ask a question but then just drops them back down into his lap.

At this point, seen from Jimmy's outdoor perspective, the high walls of Swanky's living room windows frame the front door. And, looking shell-shocked and pitifully bedraggled . . . Swanky enters . . . holding her Oscar.

Barefooted, she proceeds to the bar, gets a bottle of Jack Daniels and two champagne glasses, and comes out onto the deck where Jimmy is numb with anticipation.

Swanky fills the two glasses and hands one to Jimmy. She

then crosses the deck and leans on the railing, looking out across the ocean with her Oscar still in hand.

Jimmy waits for her to say something, anything.

Eventually, she emits a long, low, deep, primal, painful howl.

Then, suddenly, she spits roughly into the ocean.

A momentous wail follows before she turns slowly around.

Holding back a lifetime of tears, she raises her champagne glass, takes a sip, and through her sadness and despair, asks, "So, how do you think I came across?"

Jimmy looks her dead in the eye, holds his voice steady, and does his thing. "You were . . . magnificent."

Swanky takes another sip, adjusts her dress, turns back around towards the ocean, and raises her chin. "I couldn't agree with you more."

CURRENT AND UPCOMING BOOKS FROM THE "*12 STORIES FROM THE CAMPFIRES OF MY MIND*" SERIES BY DAVID CREPS

1
KING BOSS

Even if you are naturally inclined to shrug off life's constant parade of disappointments by simply denying their ultimate relevance, what's your method for disregarding a doctor's assurance that you will be dead within a month? For Johnny James, the King Boss, it meant he had one last chance to live. Finally.

(Now available on *Amazon*)

2
THE OSCAR SPEECH

This comedy set in Reno, Beverly Hills, and Malibu is the story of Best Actress nominee, Swanky Shampane, a two-timing, double-dealing, poetically-profane, ridiculously-neurotic, but fabulously charming, former cat house prostitute, obsessed with changing her public image prior to the night of the Academy Awards when she will be taking the front-row-center-seat next to her bitterest rival, "that filthy bitch" . . . Victoria Blaine.

(Now available on *Amazon*)

3
THE NEW YEAR'S RESOLUTION

A romantic comedy concerning the last two people a merciful God would ever put together under one roof, especially during the week that one of them is giving up cigarettes. It's what happens when ridiculously neurotic egos do battle while under the pressures of a calm biological attraction.

(Now available on *Amazon*)

4
THE OTHER BROTHERS

A Disney-style comedy about two twelve-year-old boys. One black. One white. One from the mean streets of Harlem, one from an isolated chicken farm in Nevada.

Both too young to be full-fledged con artists, but both already in abundant possession of the devilish charm and swagger necessary for the calling should their lives continue along their current paths.

And were it not for their love of basketball and their mutual respect for the way each other plays the game, these two big-talkers might never have made it to the brotherhood that bonds them into a lifetime of friendship.

5
MARGARITAVILLE

Is the story of two bungling con artists living on a pathetic excuse for a sailboat, in a trailer park, while looking for that one big score that will get them to the warm, turquoise waters and sandy, white beaches of the Caribbean, where they can live "just like Jimmy Buffet."

6
THE ROAD TO JACK'S HOUSE

The story of a thirty-six-year-old virgin who has a very assertive opinion on every matter under the sun. And the guy who, at the time of meeting this woman, is engaged in a search for the answer to the question, "What is the best way for me to live the rest of my life?"

They are both a little pissy, both a little self-righteous, and they each have their own personal agendas when they head down Highway 395 to take her screenplay to Hollywood, where she has good reason to believe that it will be read by Jack Nicholson. At his house. On a Saturday afternoon–while she is swimming in his pool, during a star-studded, rollicking-romp of a barbeque.

(Now available on *Amazon*)

7
LAST CHANCE

A chilling comedy about the possibilities of "what if?" What if the focus of present-day science were trained on finding a way to eliminate all violent tendencies from human behavior?

And what if a relatively small group of well-funded scientists undertook this problem, in secret, and through genetic engineering were successful in solving it?

And what if they not only discovered the formula for making humanity a passive species, but at the same time realized a way to dispense this formula throughout the world–without notice and without permission? Should they?

(Now available on *Amazon*)

8
THE GREATEST MOVIE EVER WRITTEN

The attempt by an artist of questionable sanity to write and direct a movie that will literally "save the world." The pressure is great. The time is short. And by every initial indication, his thinking is way too far "outside the box."

Yet he perseveres, fueled by a single belief: "You can't prevent the human race from destroying itself with a bigger, better weapon. But if your thoughts are crazy enough . . . you might be able to do it with an idea."

9
THE REUNION

The story of what happens when a thirty-year class reunion brings together five old high school friends who have been suffering from the same secret guilt from so many years ago.

It is also the story of what happens when Elizabeth Maryann Walker spends her weekend with these same five guys, up in the mountains, camping at Bennies Creek, falling in love for the second time in her life–with the same man.

10
THE IRONY OF IT ALL

A story of what might have happened during the last few weeks of the 2000 presidential election if the writer, Chesterfield Johnson, a man of unusual perceptions and bizarre solutions, had convinced candidate Al Gore to act in accordance with Chesterfield's unsolicited advice.

Besides his strategy to win Mr. Gore the election, Chesterfield has also devised a strategy to get his latest screenplay into the hands of an aging actress desperate to find a script worthy of her talent.

And within these dual tracks of Chesterfield's efforts, live an assortment of schemers and manipulators operating in the guise of Hollywood agents, political insiders, tabloid celebrities, and talk show hosts.

11
ON THE WALL IN THE CAVE

This comedy explores the absurdities of what can happen when a seemingly normal American man goes into a cave in the mountains to meditate on the problems of the world with the intention of figuring out the solution to the whole mess.

Current news headlines from any part of the world make this character's mindset very easy to understand.

12
THE SWEET REDEMPTION OF REPREHENSIBLE BOB

This is the story of a reprehensible human being with an insatiable need to fondle breasts at every possibility. With or without permission.

And the lovely woman who had suffered enormously for twenty years, before deciding to track him down and "shoot him through the eyeballs."

(Now available on *Amazon*)

ABOUT DAVID CREPS

David Creps has worked as a ditch-digger, truck driver, dice-dealer, carpenter, screenwriter, playwright, and novelist.

The first highlight of his writing career happened when he was twenty-two years old, and Shecky Greene read a couple pages of his stuff, and said, "I've read worse."

And, in analyzing the unspoken words within Shecky's comment, David understood Shecky to mean, "Holy crap! I am the greatest writer Shecky has ever allowed to work for him for free!"

This was enough to inspire him through decades of laborious scribbling and ultimately provide him with enough cash to get a small mortgage on a cabin 8,000 feet up in the mountains, and to purchase a genuine 1966 greenish-gray (a color occasionally referred to, behind his back, as puke-green) U.S. Postal Service mail truck lined with wall-to-wall-to-ceiling-to-floor green shag carpet, which could transport more lengths of lumber in one haul than any vehicle in this entire country.

(David is also a husband, a father, a brother, a grandfather, a good-natured, and occasionally, totally innocent, rascal.)

Made in the USA
Monee, IL
22 November 2021

82523736R00079